The Demon's Daughter

SUNY series in Hindu Studies

Wendy Doniger, editor

The Demon's Daughter
A Love Story from South India

Pingali Suranna

Translated with an Afterword by
Velcheru Narayana Rao and David Shulman

State University of New York Press

On the cover is a hand painting on cloth by Teertham Balaji, Kalamkari Artist. From the personal collection of Velcheru Narayana Rao.

Published by
State University of New York Press, Albany

© 2006 State University of New York

For information, address State University of New York Press,
194 Washington Avenue, Suite 305, Albany, NY 12210-2384

Production by Kelli Williams
Marketing by Fran Keneston

Library of Congress Cataloging-in-Publication Data

Piṅgaḷi Sūrana.
  [Prabhāvatī pradyumnamu. English]
  The demon's daughter: a love story from South India / Piṅgaḷi Sūranna; translated with an introduction by Velcheru Narayana Rao and David Shulman.
     p. cm. — (SUNY series in Hindu studies)
  Translated from Telugu.
  Includes bibliographical references and index.
  ISBN 0-7914-6695-7 (hardcover: alk. paper)
  ISBN 0-7914-6696-5 (pbk: alk. paper)
  I. Nārāyaṇarāvu, Vēlcēru, 1932– II. Shulman, David Dean, 1949– III. Title
  IV. Series.

PL4780.9.P49P713 2006
894.8'27371–dc22

                                                        2005012507

Accapu buddhiki lev' agamyamul

There is nothing beyond the grasp of an
unfettered mind.

Prabhāvatī-pradyumnamu 2.109

We dedicate this translation
to the memory of our fathers

Velcheru Buchi Narasinga Rao

Dr. Herbert Shulman

Contents

Preface

We have used the Emesco edition by Bommakanti Venkata Sing-aracarya and Balantrapu Nalinikanta Ravu (Vijayavada: M. Sesacalam and Company, 1970; reprinted 1990) as our base text, as it reflects an examination of earlier printed versions and a single manuscript (pre-pared for C. P. Brown in the early nineteenth century). No critical text is available. The *editio princeps* appeared in Madras in 1901 (Cintamani Mudraksara-sala). Purana-panda Mallayya Sastri published another edition, with gloss, in Kakinada in 1913. We have benefited greatly from the superb commentary of Vemparala Suryanarayana Sastri (Vijayavada: Venkatrama Grantha-mala, 1962/63) and from his detailed introduction.

As in our earlier translation of the *Kala-purnodayamu*, we have made no attempt to reproduce the metrical form of narrative that is, in fact, a kind of prose. Verses of a particularly lyrical flavor are trans-lated in more poetic format. We have done our best to convey some-thing of the elevated, elegant, and sometimes ironic tone of the origi-nal narrative and also to represent the individualized voices of the characters, as Suranna has fashioned them. Occasionally we have slightly shortened passages that seemed resistant to translation.[1]

Acknowledgments

We want to thank the Wissenschaftskolleg zu Berlin, which graciously provided a congenial space to work and think in the summer of 2002. We are deeply grateful to Nita Shechet and to Peter Khoroche, wise and keen-sighted readers, whose suggestions we have adopted on page after page. As always, the British Library (Oriental Printed Books and Manuscripts Reading Room) offered serendipitous pleasures. Sanjay Subrahmanyam patiently listened to much talk of talking geese. Wendy Doniger graciously invited us to submit the manuscript to her series at State University of New York Press and responded enthusiastically to the text, although she claims a novel is simply a good story well told.

Introduction

Highly original impulses often clothe themselves in available guises. In the second half of the sixteenth century, the Telugu poet Pingali Suranna composed three Telugu *kavyas* (sustained narratives in verse) in his village Krishnarayasamudramu and the small towns of Nandyala and Akuvidu in southern Andhra Pradesh, in the region that is today called Rayalasima. Each of these works, while formally continuous with the classical Telugu tradition of court poetry that reached its apogee in this period, marks a new point of departure.

We have already translated one of these three texts—the *Kala-purnodayamu*, or *The Sound of the Kiss*,[1] a subtle meditation on human emotion in relation to the creative powers of language. We have argued that this *kavya*-text is actually a novel, if by this term we mean a discursive, polyphonic, open-ended arena for the depiction of autonomous individuals endowed with complex interiority.[2] The linguistic concomitants of this new form are clearly present in Suranna's other work, the *Raghava-pandaviyamu*, which simultaneously tells the story of the two great epics, *Mahabharata* and *Ramayana*. Such dense intralinguistic playfulness becomes one major vector in the development of Telugu poetry in this period.[3] The contrasting vector, very pronounced in the *Kala-purnodayamu*, takes us toward more directly narrative and novelesque modes, in effect using metrical forms to read like prose. The *Prabhavati-pradyumnamu*, translated here, is a striking example of this new trend.

The history of Telugu literature, like that of many others, has a rather oblique relation to the domains of politics, state-building, and war. The "imperial" edifice of Vijayanagara that had supported such great poets as Peddana and the famous poet-king Krishna-deva-raya in the early sixteenth century had largely collapsed after 1565. Political power was scattered among small rival kingdoms throughout the

southern Deccan, including the Akuvidu and Nandyala courts where
Suranna was active. In these remote, miniature polities, often ruled by
self-made men drawn from communities newly emergent on the political scene, intellectual and artistic life could be very intense. These little kings often depended more on their poets than vice versa: the poet
held in his hands, or on his tongue, the ruler's tenuous hope for fame
and status. For their part, multilingual poets and their audiences created a communicative space that connected disparate locales and cultural milieux, a space in which there was room for remarkable experimentation and innovation.[4]

Suranna's period was one of rapid social and structural change.
We have elsewhere documented the rise of a highly mobile, nonascrip-
tive elite capable of maneuvering successfully within the unstable
political realm and of manipulating (cumulating and investing) the
increasingly available free-floating resources.[5] Throughout the eastern
Deccan, during the late sixteenth and seventeenth centuries, Velama
and Reddi lineages, as well as warriors from farther afield (Karnataka,
Bundelkhand, and even as far north as Afghanistan), were carving out
more or less autonomous states within a wider system still partly
dominated by the last, displaced (Aravidu) dynasty of Vijayanagar
and by its major rivals the Golconda and Bijapur Sultanates to the
north.[6] European powers were also beginning to impinge on these
polities from their footholds on the coasts. But in the interior, in the
small towns and royal courts of Rayalasima, a characteristic Deccani
ethos survived, rooted in memories of even earlier, Kakatiya-period
cultural forms—an ethos of rugged individuals bound in ties of personal loyalty to their overlord, claiming individual ownership of lands
and proclaiming the unique status of their lineage by building or
patronizing large-scale, clan-based temples.[7] These men were warriors
and entrepreneurs, a somewhat surprising amalgam motivated by
exemplary stories of singular achievement and endowed with a particular form of historical awareness.[8] They tended to patronize poets
who were capable of articulating a novel, experimental vision, rich in
political implications, that adapted earlier imperial idioms to the
volatile context of the late sixteenth-century Rayalasima courts.

Suranna is an outstanding instance of this experimental trend
that generated new expressive modes and distinctive templates of
perception.[9] We can see indications of far-reaching change in every
major cultural domain: in the refashioning of the political order and
the attempts to reimagine its metaphysical basis;[10] in the rise of "left-

hand" temple cults and their eventual takeover of important pilgrimage sites such as Lepaksi and, above all, Tirupati;[11] in a cash-oriented economy and its concomitant effects on the vision of the social order;[12] in a newly crystallizing anthropology, including a revised understanding of gender identities and relations; and in the emergence, in a variety of expressive media (painting, sculpture, and a shifting literary ecology and system of genres), of what is arguably an altered, protomodern sense of self. Let us repeat: we often find powerful conceptual novelty making use of familiar, available materials. Thus Suranna borrowed the story he tells from the *Hari-vamsa*, an ancient *purāṇa*-like compendium of stories related to Krishna and appended to the *Mahabharata*.[13] On the whole, he follows the inherited story line remarkably closely. Nonetheless, the entire texture of telling has been so radically transformed that both the characters and the meaning of the story are no longer the same. What we see in Suranna's *Prabhavati* is a statement of love as individualized and individualizing emotion animating a psychologically integrated subject. In addition, the poet offers trenchant statements and images about the role of art and imagination in creating various types of reality.

Here are the bare bones of this love story, which fits the *Romeo and Juliet* pattern. An *asura* antigod, Vajranabha, has built an impenetrable city, Vajrapuri. No one—not even the wind—can enter or leave without his permission. From this vantage point, Vajranabha has invaded and occupied Amaravati, the city of the gods and their king, Indra. His intention is to take over the divine kingdom entirely and replace Indra as world ruler. In despair, Indra pleads with Krishna to send help and reinforcements. But how can anyone even approach the hermetically sealed Vajrapuri? After watching a troupe of actors, Krishna suddenly has a bright idea. He could, perhaps, infiltrate an agent into the demons' city in the guise of an actor.[14] But this actor may need a little personal motivation apart from the great matters of cosmopolitics.

Krishna has a son named Pradyumna, a reincarnation of the god of desire, Manmatha or Kama. In Indra's mind, Pradyumna is the right candidate for this mission. To provide extra incentive, Indra orders an extremely articulate female goose named Sucimukhi, "Perfect Speech," to make Pradyumna fall in love with Vajranabha's exquisite daughter, Prabhavati. For her part, Prabhavati has already fallen in love, at a distance, with Pradyumna because of a painting that the goddess Parvati gave her in a dream. Similar budding romances bind Pradyumna's companions Gada and Samba to two other girls in Vajrapuri: Candravati and Gunavati. Our novel spells out the ins and outs of this dangerous secret mission.

The matchmaking goose Sucimukhi already inhabits the *Hari-vamsa* "parent"-text, as do the actors in whose guise Krishna's team enters the forbidden city.[15] But while the *Hari-vamsa* text tells a fast-paced, hard-hitting story that is ultimately another episode in the eternal war between gods and antigods, for Suranna the narrative frame serves mostly to develop a subtle, personal exploration of the experiences and sensations of falling in love and being in love. This love is of a type that seems never to have been documented before in Indian literature.

To this end, Suranna has invented various episodes and devices.[16] The goose Sucimukhi's persona is vastly expanded beyond the *Hari-vamsa* portrayal, to the point where she effectively master-minds the unfolding plot and, at the same time, continuously comments on the moods and concerns of its major players. Both articulate speech, embodied in this bird, and plastic and performing arts become central to the story and to the psychology of its characters. Pradyumna's portrait, painted by the goddess Parvati, has no precedent in the Sanskrit version of the story. We also have a crucial love letter—probably the first of its kind in South Indian literature—that provides the main structural node of this novel. And while the overt forms of the narration may appear, at first glance, to preserve the somewhat extreme habits of earlier Indian lovers, readers should attune their ears to the gently ironic tone of Suranna's metrical prose. This poet is telling us something unusual: not only about love but also about the life of the imagination in general, and about the ways an artist has of making something, or someone, real. We discuss these themes at length in the afterword; but please read the story first.

The Demon's Daughter

A Love Story from South India

Chapter One

Prayers

Uma and Siva
became two halves of a single body
because they wished to show each other
how thin they'd grown
from missing one another
when they lived apart.
Their love is ever new.
May that loving couple bring fame
to the lord of this book.

Couples love each other
because of Love.
That same Love was born
to the Ancient Couple,
Vishnu and Lakshmi.[1]
None can equal their togetherness.
May they bless my father, Amaresa Mantri,
son of Pingali Surana,[2]
with every joy.

The Goddess of Speech and the Creator
enhance with their own colors
the white and gold of the goose
they ride. To those who believe in them

they give silver and gold, fame and power,
whenever asked, as if they held in their hands
all the wealth of their creation—
for my father Amara.

My Family

After praising the three ancient couples who cause the world to revolve, I was thinking of the first poets, Valmiki and Vyasa, as I began to compose a very remarkable work, the *Prabhavati-pradyumnamu*. One day I thought to myself that, although I had composed the *Garuda-puranamu*, the *Raghava-pandaviyamu*, the *Kala-purnodayamu*, and any number of other Telugu books, none of them gave me satisfaction—since none of them includes any history of my family, beginning with my father.

The Veda tells us that a father is a god to his children. So how can I fail to offer worship to my father, as other sons do? My younger brother Errana performed death-offerings to our father in Gaya, Kasi, Prayaga, Srisailam, Haridvara, the Blue Mountain [Puri], Ujjayini, Dvaraka, Ayodhya, Mathura, the Naimisa Forest, and Kuruksetra. I thought I too should do something to honor him. I can give him a book and establish his fame in this world forever, through the grace of God.

Having decided, I began to compose the *Prabhavati-pradyumnamu*, with my father's name on it. For an auspicious opening, I will now describe my family's history.

A profound sage brought a branch of the Ganges to this world and called it by his name. He was Gautama, a great ascetic. Siva himself, unable to conquer him in debate, opened his burning third eye; Gautama, in turn, revealed an eye on his foot. He composed the textbook of logic with its scientific criteria for argument.

In his line was born the famous Gokana of Pingali town. He made a *gandharvi* called Peki his servant because he was a great Yogi.[3] He became famous with his poem on Visnu's sword.[4] Having no children, his wife prayed to the Sun. He came to her in a dream and gave her a *donda* vine, promising that she would become fruitful through it. The family expanded and flourished with children and grandchildren for many generations, like a vine spreading far and wide.

If people live in the same village for four or five generations, the family genealogy is forgotten, and they are known only by the name of their village. That's what happened to our family. Gokamantri's descendents were all called Pingalis. Some, like Pingali Ramaya and others, lived on the banks of the Gautami and Krsna rivers. Some, like Pingali Gadaya and others, lived in Palanadu and Pakanadu. As for me, living here,[5] we are all known to be descended from the same Pingali Goka.

In that great family, the illustrious branch that produced my father is as follows: A certain Gangaya, as pure as Ganga, was born. He had three sons: Suranna, Kupanna, and Ramana. Kuppana had a son called Surana. His sons were Papaya, Bhadrana, and Kupparya. Their sons were Erraya and Papaya. They were wise.

As for Ramana, his son was Gangana, whose son was Gadana, who produced Peddaya and several other sons.

Surana, son of Gangaya, was much admired by his brothers and their offspring. Because he had the lotus sign of royalty on the soles of his feet, kingship came to him. He had the honor of being carried in a palankeen and fanned by yak-tail whisks. No lord was equal to him except the lord of heaven. He was so generous that those who begged from him became donors in their own right. This Surana's son was also Suraya.[6] Lions give birth only to lions.

That Suraya married Akkamamba and had four noble sons: Annaya, Suraya, Vallaya, and Linganarya. Vallaya had Pullaya, and Lingana's sons were Suraya and Akkaya. Suraya's son, Suraya, was a poet, devoted to Siva. He married Amalamba, daughter of Velagaleti Amaramatya. They had three sons: Amaresvara, Mallana, and Akkana. Mallana had five sons: Jaggana, Tammaya, Suraya, Cinnaya, and Timmaya.

Amaresvara, otherwise known as Amaranarya, was my father. He married Ambamma, my mother, who came from a long and honorable line. Her great-grandfather was Ciruvana Deciraju. Her grandfather was Kesayya. Her father was Bhavayya, brother to Annayya and Bapayya. My mother's brothers are Kondayya and Raghavayya. Her elder uncle's son is Kesayya, and her younger uncle's son is Gangayya. Her mother, my maternal grandmother, was Annamma,[7] the daughter of Racapudi Ganapati.

We are three brothers: myself, Amararya, and Errana. We also have a sister who gave birth to a son, Racapudi Gangana.

VERSES OF OFFERING

To the diadem of this famous family
who was equipped with both sword and supreme insight
(the latter in his head, the former in his hand)—
both serving to protect the dharma—
brilliant as the rising sun,
born in the Gautama lineage,
in the Apastamba sūtra and the Yajus branch of the Veda,
who conquered his inner enemies by profound self-control,
whose name is known from Kasi to the Bridge,[8]
whose sons feed many people in their village,
Nidumanuru, also known as Krishnarayasamudram,

to him who is pure as the Ganga,
his fame untouched by slander,
whose loving son is Pingali Surana,

to the son of Amalamba and husband of Ambamma,
to my father, Amaramatya, who is like the Creator himself
and who is honored by honoring scholars,
who has gone beyond illusion by meditating on Siva,
who floats on the flood of immortality,

to him, wishing him an endless good name, I offer my book, Prabhavati-
*   pradyumnamu. Here we begin.*

DVARAKA, WHERE THE STORY OPENS

   Krishna, the god with the brilliant goddess on his breast, was living in Dvaraka. One day Indra came down from heaven to see him in
order to discuss some matter of importance to the world. As he was
descending through the sky, he observed the city from a distance:

like the central brooch in the waistband of ocean
worn by the goddess Earth,
like the dot on the forehead of Siva, who is the earth,
with the ocean wrapped as a turban round his head,
like a blossom painted on the edge of the ocean
that is the sari worn by the Woman of the Western Sky,

like a bouquet of flowers draped over the gateway to
   Varuna's watery city.[9]
Precious stones lit up house after house, as far as you could see.

Indra's thousand eyes could hardly take it all in. Matali, his charioteer, watched him shaking his head at the beauty of this city. With
the hint of a smile in his eyes, the charioteer said,

"Why are you so surprised? So there's a city on earth that's amazing
to the god from the sky. This city is like a dancer just emerged from
behind the curtain that is the ocean to entice and delight. Or she is
the Goddess perched between dark ocean and dark forests, like
Lakshmi on Vishnu's breast.

You know what I think? The snake Sesha
could not bear to be separated from Vishnu
when the god became Krishna in Dvaraka,
so he came down himself and turned his coils
into winding walls and the jewels in his thousand hoods
into gleaming palaces.

Colored by light from gems set in the banners
that people have pinned to the top of palaces, the clouds
cannot be distinguished from these flags
until they move on a little ways, and now
you wonder if they're really clouds at all and not dark
columns of aloe incense reaching into the sky.

Indra! Look carefully. Not even an expert can be sure, unless he goes
very close, that he's looking at an emerald floor in a house studded
with rubies and not at a mango grove, lush green leaves sprinkled
with bright red buds.

King of the gods! Have a look at the love-garden inside
   the palace.
It looks like Siva in all its parts. The pleasure mound of silver
imitates the body of the god. A grove of campaka flowers,
orange and black, suggests the tiger's skin he wears.
Steps built from sapphires spiral upwards like
   his black snakes.

There is a fence made from coral vines, like his matted hair.
A little lake could be the Ganges he carries, and the rowboat
      floating there
is the crescent moon on his head.

Algae trembling in the water look like whole gardens in movement. Rippling high waves are walking fortresses, thick white foam
on the shore—uprooted palaces washed with lime. The fine spray
from the water is a shower of pearls given in tribute. As the breeze
from all directions stirs the waters of the moat, you can almost see a
series of enemy cities rushing to pay homage to Dvaraka, at the
king's command.

People who know say that the ocean is to the west. Other than
that, there's no way of telling the moats on all four sides of the city
from the high sea.

Young women flash through the dark pleasure gardens.
Thunderclouds, with their dull lightning,
have every reason to be ashamed. Still they come, brazen,
toward this city. And if they didn't?
What's there to lose? There's more than enough honey
flowing in streams from the flowers
to water whatever grows."

INDRA'S DISTRESS

Indra and his charioteer went on bantering like this, to their
own delight, as different parts of the city came into view. After some
distance they came down to earth and began walking toward the city
grounds. Krishna heard they had come and summoned his beloved
brother, Satyaki, to welcome the King of the Gods. Satyaki took an
appropriate retinue, met Indra, and showed him the way into the city
via the entrance towers that were decorated with fresh banana
plants, inseparable from emerald pillars. On either side of the royal
road there were festive arches bursting into life whenever extremely
beautiful women looked in their direction. As they reached the
entrance of Krishna's palace, Krishna himself came out of the inner
courtyards together with Ugrasena, Vasudeva, Sankarshana, Gada,
Akrura, and others, and received him as is proper. They greeted one

another with mounting excitement and mutual courtesy; they inquired about one another's wellbeing. Now Indra said to Krishna,

"I'm well, now that I have the privilege
of seeing you. I don't have to elaborate
on that, do I, Krishna? As to how I was
before, you're God, there's nothing
you don't know. To say I was well
would be a lie.

Still, if you want to hear it from my mouth, just listen and pay attention, Krishna. I'll tell you all the heaviness of my heart. This monster Vajranabha made friends with Brahma, the Creator, by means of strict inner discipline. Brahma built him a city called Vajrapuri, near Mount Meru, a city no one can enter, not even the wind or the sun, without permission. Aflame with arrogance, Vajranabha embarked on a life of pleasure and splendor.

The other day, in his blindness, he invaded my city. How can I describe his crudeness? He thought me worth even less than a blade of grass. He sent his armies to camp out in Nandana Garden, where every bud has been nurtured by water poured from the delicate hands of my exquisite courtesans.

Can the wishing trees stand it when these monsters climb on
them and kick them and break their branches?
Can they bear it when rotten, leftover human flesh is spread
all over them?
Can they survive being made into tying-posts for elephants?
Can they suffer the filthy, sweat-soaked clothes these
cannibals hang on them?
When these thoughts—the horrible things this demon did to
my lovely garden—come to my mind, I burn with grief.

Not one among the gods was capable of standing up to him. This was part of the boon Brahma gave him. (I was so tormented that I forgot to mention it before.) That's why he was able to do whatever he pleased. Brihaspati, my guru, and I talked about it. We sent him a message, saying, 'We shouldn't fight among ourselves. After all, we're cousins. You should listen to us, and we should listen to you.

That's how we can live in peace.' So, all too aware of the limits of our power, and in the hope of calming the situation, we invited him as a member of the family into our town and gave him and his army living quarters equal to ours.

Now, when some nameless rascal of a demon complains that I didn't give him enough, I have to grovel and appease him. If some idiot curses me for not sending Rambha[10] to his bed, I fold my hands in reverence. Another lowlife creature asks why I didn't respect him before all this, and I have to offer him worship. Some deadhead tells me off for not serving him the drink of life, and I have to be nice to him. Listen, God. What *I* have to suffer no one would put up with. I figure that only some sinful animal could be promoted to Indra's job.

I may look normal to you, Krishna
since my pain has been relieved, for the moment,
by seeing the unearthly beauties of your astonishing city.
But believe me, I've lost my usual glow.

Anyway, let this be. I've tried to treat him with all due respect. Still, one day that marauding demon came with all his forces, armed to the teeth, and stood in my doorway. He sent word that he had something to discuss with me. I sent suitable people to bring him in; but his troops, heavy as boulders, smashed their way into the palace, trampling the doorkeepers. Ahead of them marched Vajranabha, cocky, full of himself, and took his seat on my own throne.

His men grabbed all the sages in the court and, pulling them by their arms, threw them out. Then they occupied all the sages' seats, unopposed. Great ascetics and gods were stupefied and withdrew, swallowing their words.

My only thought at that moment was that there was no way to say yes or no. I started to worry that this angry monster might capture me and my guru. There was nothing to stop him. A true disaster. I was scared. But I pretended to be calm so that he would not sense my fear. I gathered my dignity and ordered my servants to bring him gifts of clothes and jewels. Seeing this flurry, he, my inveterate enemy, said, 'Enough. I'm pleased. But—*I* should be king here. *I* should enjoy all these fine things and give them to whomever I like. Why should I have to put up with waiting for someone else to make a gift?

'You've been rather nice to me all these days so, out of courtesy, I didn't complain. I didn't realize how tricky you are. I'll tell

you one thing, if you're an honest man. I don't need any more of
your fake friendship.

'I want to rule this kingdom for as long
as you have, sitting on this throne.
It's only fair. We're all children
of the same father, Kasyapa,
aren't we? Admit it. Get the hell
out of here.

'If you won't, Mr. Indra,
you know you're all in my hands.
Why waste words? I'll throw you in prison
right now.' I smiled

and answered, 'Why talk of prison?
Think of living together like friends.
This isn't the moment to rush into
breaking up the family.
You're a good man.

'Just as you said,' I continued, 'we're both sons of the same
father. He should settle our disputes. Let's go to that great sage.
If he says I should give you the throne, I'll do so. From the beginning you've been patient and heard me out. Is it right for a strong
person like you to lose patience at this point? Can a sweet mouth
taste bitter food?'

"I went on and on like this and eventually got him to agree. I
couldn't see any other way out. So, gathering up Brihaspati and whoever else was there among my people, I went with him to Kasyapa.
This venerable sage was busy with a sacrifice. He said he would listen to our dispute only when the ritual was complete. In the mean-
time, he pacified the enemy of the gods and told him to go home to
his city, Vajrapuri.

Surprisingly, the demon agreed. We were lucky.
Thanks to that sage, we escaped danger,
like meat pulled from a tiger's teeth.
We went home very slowly, touching our heads
to make sure they were still there.

But we don't know when he'll hit us again after lulling us into relaxing. As for me, I've given up all hope of getting back my kingdom. Even if you pour wealth as high as I stand, I won't take a single step in that direction. I'm too scared. I'll just stay here, if you don't mind, Krishna, serving you."

Krishna covered his ears with both hands.

"That's not fair. How could you want to be a servant? You're king of all the gods. Carts go on boats, and boats on carts.[11] Relatives need one another from time to time. There's nothing unusual about wanting to stay in a friendly house. Why so many words?

If you think it through, haven't many demons
grown so powerful they thought they were invincible?
What happened to them in the end, Indra?
They're all dead. The days of this one, too,
are numbered. He caused you
so much pain, but he can't get away with hurting
a good man.

At the moment, my father Vasudeva is bent on carrying out a major ritual. It's for your sake as well. As soon as that ceremony is finished, from that day on, we will focus our minds only on punishing that demon, boons and all. Meanwhile, keep looking for ways to take him on. This is no small matter. Find out how to get into his city, and who can stand up to him."

With this, Krishna sent Indra off and went back to managing his father's rite.

The earth was enriched with particles of gold when ornaments worn by kings from all the countries of the world rubbed and chafed against each other. Water was enriched by flooding streams from the final ritual bath. Fire was enriched with oblations poured out with ringing chants. Air was enriched with the fragrance of milk and curds mixed together. The sky was enriched with the smoke of the offerings. Vasudeva's sacrificial rite enhanced all the elements.

Rituals become effective when you mention Vishnu's name, and now that god, the Imperishable, the First, the Lotus-Eyed, came himself for all to see, to protect this rite. When it was over and Krishna was busy honoring his royal relatives and all the friends

who had come from the ends of the earth, an actor named Bhadra
arrived and astonished everyone with his skill. The sages assembled
there, very taken by him, gave him boons; others gave him fine
clothes and ornaments. Bhadra took all this and praised each of the
donors in some special way.

There were, however, some mischievous Brahmin teenagers[12]
who, as a joke, threw him the spare loincloths they were carrying,
tied to a walking stick. "Bhadra," they cried, winking to one another.
"Sing our praises, too. That's why we're offering you this precious
gift." Smiling, Bhadra rolled the loincloths into a ball, tossed them
high into the sky and caught them, again and again, as they fell while
he yelled in a deep voice, "Ohoho!

"You are the unfolding buds of Brahmin families
that spread the fragrance of the Veda.
You are sparks of the inner fire that purifies the world.
Though you're small as pegs on a wall, you're strong enough
to reach Brahma's head.
You're smart, the standard yardstick for lies and loud words.
Young students, acting out Vishnu's role as the Dwarf[13]—
your sumptuous gift has brought all our plans to fruition."

They laughed and replied, somewhat aggressively,

"Hey, Actor. This kind of noise is not praise.
We don't like it. We shouldn't take back
the loincloths you've touched with your hands,
but we won't go away without them."

They wouldn't leave. They surrounded him. He tried to control them
with smiles and with anger. He looked at his troupe of actors: "These
kids are trying to steal our costumes. Watch out. They're thieves."
This excited the boys, who protested.

"You call us thieves? People like you
are the real source of thievery.
You gain entrance to any city with ease,
because you're actors. All day long
you delude people with your plays.
You take note of alleys and backroads,
and at night you burgle your way into houses.
If anyone tries to stop you, you strike them down.

Quiet as dead lice, you take whatever you fancy.
That's your usual way of life, as everyone knows."

Krishna, meanwhile, was still thinking about Indra's problem.
He was looking for a way to enter Vajrapuri to make war. Now he
had the solution, in the Brahmin boys' words. After all, Vishnu advises following whatever a Brahmin says.[14]

God took a hint from the boys[15] and decided that, with this strategy, someone could easily enter Vajrapuri and destroy the demon. He
was wondering who would be the right person for the job.

INTRODUCING SUCIMUKHI THE GOOSE

Meanwhile, Indra was also searching for some means of
destroying the demon. He summoned the geese who play serenely in
the River in the Sky. Very serious, he addressed them.

"Listen, geese! There's an emergency, and we need your help.
If you can manage this task, your life will have been well lived. Let
me explain.

"You know very well how much trouble our enemy, this
Vajranabha, has caused us. I don't have to elaborate. We're now
determined to kill him. This is a secret. If it gets out, it will cause
harm, so keep it to yourselves. We can't tell what he might do to out-
wit us. We want you to move carefully through his city, spying for
me. Your mission is to gather intelligence about whatever happens in
that city day after day, and to convey it to us. No one else can do it.
Not even the Wind can get into the city without his permission, let
alone anyone else. But the demon king enjoys your comings and
goings. You grace his pools and ponds. In fact, there's no one who
doesn't like watching you."

At this point a certain goose, husband to Sucimukhi, came to a
halt before Indra and said, his face aglow, "Lord, as of now, that
monster Vajranabha is so blind with conceit and power that he does-
n't know himself. In my opinion, he will not come back at you—not
now, not ever. Still, one should not be complacent when it comes to
the gods' affairs. A few of us have just returned from Vajrapuri. My
wife says that his wealth and rule have run their course. She can tell
you all that herself." He summoned her, introduced her to Indra, and
said, "Tell the king what you said to me about the impending end of
Vajranabha's kingdom. Don't leave anything out."

Sucimukhi faced Indra and said,

"For a long time we've been going to his city—
because we're silly, and we're hungry, too.
Forgive us, lord, for this fault.
After all, we're only birds.
Strictly speaking, those who visit an enemy kingdom
can't be your friends.

But how can we not go there?

He's stolen the best of the golden lotuses from the Ganges
*   in the sky.*
He's raided Manasa Lake, which we call 'Good Heart,' and
*   made it 'Heartless.'*[16]
He's dug up the golden lotuses in Bindu Lake, leaving
*   not one behind.*
Nothing but water is left in the great pond called Saugandhika. It's
*   ruined.*
He's transplanted all the finest varieties of lotus to his own pleasure
*   pools, and left*
all other places empty.
If we don't go there, where else can we geese find food?

That's how it is. We sought Vajranabha's permission to roam freely
through all the water sources of his kingdom—lakes, ponds, tanks,
pools, wells. He agreed because we bring beauty to water. Yesterday,
as we were frolicking in a pond in the inner palace where the young
girls live, we overheard a radiant young woman, like regal beauty
incarnate, talking to a friend in private, hidden behind a flowering
gurivenda bush on the shore.

Prabhavati's Dream

'My friend,' she said, 'let me tell you the dream I dreamt
*   before dawn.*
I'm still amazed whenever I think of it. It's not at all
the kind of dream people usually see or hear.
It's partly a dream, and partly real.' Then she was too shy
*   to go on.*

'You took an oath never to keep a secret from me. There are no hidden things between us.' Her friend was insistent, and at last she relented.

'The goddess Parvati came to me in my dream.
She was friendly, and a gentle smile
flowered on her face. Kindly
she called me to her. She stroked my body
with one hand as she said, 'I've found a husband
*   for you.'*

She produced, just by thinking, a flat board
and proceeded to paint on it the image
of a young man of striking beauty, dignity,
energy, and other surpassing qualities.
'Here's your husband,' she said, 'a prince.
His name is Pradyumna. A son born
to the two of you will rule this city.'
That's what she said. The elders who were there
told me to bow to her, so I did, and sent her off.
That was the dream, but the real part of it is
this picture, right here.'

That's exactly what I overheard, Indra," said Sucimukhi. "That's why I decided in my mind that Vajranabha's rule is near its end. But you should think it through yourself.

Take it from me. Parvati's promise—
that this young girl will marry Pradyumna—
can't be untrue.
Believe me. That monster Vajranabha
will never willingly give his daughter
to the son of his enemy.
Trust me. If Pradyumna is to marry Prabhavati,
there's certain to be war.
Rest assured. If Prabhavati's son is to rule the city,
Vajranabha has to die.

Since the painting is there for us to see,
the dream is credible. And because it came

right before dawn, it will come true very soon.
Think it over, God, for yourself.

I learned from the conversation between those girls, after the dream was told, that the princess is Prabhavati, and that she is Vajranabha's daughter. I'll give you some further details. They might be useful for your plans." So she spoke, the sweetness of her voice intensified by her earnestness, and Indra listened with rapt attention.

"As soon as she finished reporting the dream, the girlfriend said in wonder, shaking her head, 'What a lucky girl you are. You were born through the blessing of Parvati and your mother's inner discipline. Now *you* have won Parvati's admiration. No one can rival you.

'If the goddess born from the mountain, who came to you in a dream, didn't love you, would she have painted this picture for you, so you could see your husband right before you? Let me tell you, this picture has turned up in a place that can't be entered by any male, even a fly. Your father won't like it.

'He's so jealous that he boils without fire. You think he'll accept this? He'll punish us first, saying that some woman brought this picture into the palace by pretending to be Parvati. If anyone catches sight of that painting, the news will spread. Everyone will talk. If anyone asks *me*, I haven't seen it.

Hurry, before the others come.
Bring the picture fast, from wherever
you hid it. Until I see with my own eyes
what the goddess painted, my mind will know
no rest. Whom did she paint?
It would be almost impossible to find,
in all creation, some man suited to your
perfect beauty.'

The princess said, 'I've hidden it right here, behind this bush.' She at once brought it out and, together, they removed the cloth that covered it.

He was smiling. Looking at them
with wide eyes, as if about to strike up
a conversation with them. That picture
the goddess painted was so alive

with depth and feeling that Prabhavati
and her friend were too shy to look straight at it.

After all, it's only a picture—so she lifts her head
to take a look. But no, it's real—
so at once she turns aside.
Battling shyness, she wants
another look. Then she feels
her husband touching her with his eyes,
so she forces her eyes away.

Bringing fear and shyness and all other impediments under some
minimal control, and now certain that it was only a picture, she took
a long, careful look at her husband. Her girlfriend also studied the
picture with much amazement.

'Such beauty can't exist in the world.
The goddess must have painted him
from her imagination. But this can't be right.
The Creator made him first and then,
so he'd have a companion, he created you.'

'It's nice of you to say that. But tell me truly.
If it's not just some skill in painting,
is it possible that such a man exists for real
somewhere in the world? If so, I swear
I'm not fit to be a slave at his feet.'

You could see she was already in love. And you can easily
imagine that this woman will make every effort to bring Pradyumna
to her, fast. It seems to me that all this might just help you in your
plans," the goose concluded. Indra was listening with avid interest.

━┼━━━0━━━┼━

His erudition adorned the earth.
His eyes were cool with compassion,
but the red tinge at their corners was enough

to burn away his enemies' pride.
His fame lives on, ever young, in his children and
     grandchildren.
Such was my father.

━┥━◆━O━◆━┝━

This is the first chapter in the book called *Prabhavati-pradyumnamu*,
composed by Suraya, son of Pingali Amaranarya. All great scholars
celebrate his poetry and sing of his modesty.

Chapter Two

 *Amaranarya, son of Suraya, spread
the fame of his Gautama clan
far and wide.*

THE GOOSE'S COMMISSION

Indra, god of a thousand eyes,[1] was even more impressed by the
goose's careful choice of words than by her potential usefulness to
him. He enjoyed her eloquence for its own sake; it gave him a new,
quite unexpected kind of pleasure. He said to her,

"You prevent even the slightest slippage
from the definitive nature of the word.
You let the richness of meaning arise
from the way you combine words.
What you intend comes through unmarred
and luminous. You avoid repetition.
You follow through as the anticipation inherent
in the sentence requires. You don't jump
from branch to branch. You connect things
in such a way that the primary focus is fully grounded.
Whatever logic is in play comes out in all
its force, without conflict between what you say first
and what you say later. All the individual parts
and subplots, each with its own meanings,
fit well with the larger statement.
That's what speaking really means.
It's your great gift.

There's no one to compare with you.
Given your expertise with words,
you're no bird. You're either the goddess
of speech herself, or some fine-feathered
poet that she has trained."

"Your second guess is right," replied the bird.
"O king: You're a god.
You captured it all when you called me a 'trained poet'.[2]
When a wise person thinks a word through,
no meaning can slip away.

I'm the daughter of a goose named Sarandhara, who pulls Brahma's chariot. I was raised by the goddess Speech herself, and she taught me all her skills."

Indra understood. "So that's why you have this facility with words. Another goddess—Luck—has brought you my way at this critical moment, when I'm not able to find a way out of my misery. No one but you can bring the gods' mission to fruition. I beg you: keep going back to Vajrapuri as usual, with your flock. Play in the waters of the pleasure pools, but seek a way to make friends with Prabhavati. Describe Pradyumna to her in such a way that she can't help but fall in love with him. Make it possible for them to meet and make love as soon as possible. But first go to Dvaraka and tell Krishna that I have sent you. Tell him the whole plan. Take his advice."

Indra turned to the other geese. "All of you must follow *her* lead and do whatever she asks of you. It's for the good of the gods."

He sent them off, and the goose went happily,
intent on the gods' mission. If you think about it,
it's always useful to have a noble goose on your side.[3]
There's a certain beauty in relying on someone beautiful.

She went there. She spotted Krishna from a distance, surrounded by all eight of his wives. He was resting in a pavilion by the lake. "This is the moment to approach him," she thought, so with the rest of the flock she came down from the sky straight into the lake, which sprang to life in a flurry of golden wings.

She approached Krishna,whose head was resting on Rukmini's thighs while Satyabhama stroked his feet. Bhadra was fanning him, while Mitravinda held the yak-tail whisk. Kalindi was ready with the spitoon as Jambavati offered him folded leaves with betel. Nagnajit had his sandals ready at hand, and Laksana carried a pot of water.

The picture was complete. Krishna, wives,
lotuses, pond, and goose. A dark raincloud
graced with flashes of lightning. A sky lit up
with stars and in the middle, the radiant moon.

The bird approached without fear, to the women's great surprise. Looking at Krishna, she said, "I have a message for you from Indra." Then she added, "I need to speak with you in private." She thought Rukmini might not like the idea of her son going to battle with a demon.

Krishna was quite taken by the bird's eloquence, obvious intelligence, and artistry. A gentle smile danced on his cheeks. He moved his head from Rukmini's thighs and his feet from Satyabhama's lap. Sitting up, he picked the betel leaves Jambavati was offering with his own glowing hands. The women understood and moved away.

Now that Krishna had granted privacy, the goose told the whole story beginning from the moment Indra had summoned her and ending with his order to fly to Krishna, repeating every word that had passed between them.

Krishna was glad. He already had a clear idea
of what to do, taking his hint from what the Brahmin boys
had said. Now the rest of the plan came into focus
through the words of the bird. The right person
to bring about Vajranabha's death had been found.

He said to Sucimukhi,

"Pradyumna is strong, courageous,
and better at magic than the demons
themselves. From what you say I can see
that he'll be the right man to marry Prabhavati,
and Vajranabha is sure to die at his hands.

We know that no one can get into that demon's city without permission. I'll tell you how Pradyumna will manage it. There's an actor named Bhadra, who came here at the time my father was holding a sacrifice. He performed for the sages, and they granted him invincibility, easy mobility across all seven continents, the ability to fly, and an actor's dream—when he acts, no one will be able to tell him apart from the role. Now he's traveling, showing off the full power of his art. You have to get the demon king interested in him, so that he'll be invited into the city. Then Pradyumna will arrive looking just like him.

This is your mission. You will know whatever else is necessary to achieve it. Go. Do it for the gods." He sent her off. The goose flew into the sky with her companions in the direction of Vajrapuri.

The Goose Visits Pradyumna

As they passed over Dvaraka, they looked down and saw Pradyumna outside the city, playing a game on horseback.

He hit a ball into the sky with a golden bat, and the horse ran forward, backward, sideways, wherever the ball would fall so he could hit it again, almost as if he could read his rider's mind. Afterward Pradyumna thought it was too easy like this; he started throwing the ball ahead of him and racing the horse toward it, to hit it again before it touched the earth. The brilliant gems on the bat seemed to penetrate the ball with light. He made the horse circle round. At first it looked like a single horse making a circuit; then as if there were many similar horses circling together. Then it looked like a single mass, out of focus, spinning rapidly; and at last, it was a circle of light, for you could see only the whirling ornaments. As the speed increased, people nearby left what they were doing and cried out to him, "Sir! Take care! Hold the reins tight!" The horse circled like a firebrand, fast as the potter's wheel, and Krishna's son rode it as the central spit turns the wheel. He exhausted the horse with the five different ways of holding the reins, as the earrings he wore jumped and shook in unison. Satisfied with these exertions, Pradyumna reined in the horse just as it was stretching its front legs upward and standing on its hind legs, as if about to compete with the horses that carry the sun through the sky. He patted the horse and rubbed its back to cool its strength. Its neck bent back under the force of the reins, and its muzzle was bruised by the bit; the saddle was covered with foam on either side.

He dismounted as his groom held the stirrup. A friend took his hand, while others waved gems and clothes to ward off the evil eye. Looking down at him from above, Sucimukhi said aloud, so he could hear her, "This must be the man. We should go and talk to him." She wanted to surprise him. Together with the other geese, she came down for a landing.

As they descended from the sky, they were lovely beyond any description. They were like white cloth with golden borders given by the gods as a reward for this particular horseman's skill. They were like fame itself, a white solid mass enveloping the superb rider. They were like white clouds streaked with golden lightning that came begging for a still richer whiteness—the foam flowing from the horse's mouth. Or you could say that the Ganges was spilling pollen from its golden lotus flowers because the horse as it circled had put its whirlpools to shame.

Approaching the ground in a slanting formation, they hovered a while, their wings still; they flew past Pradyumna, then returned, puffing up their breasts; then, flapping their wings, they planted their feet on the ground and folded the wings inward, twisting their heads very elegantly to preen their exquisite plumage, white feathers flecked with gold.

Pradyumna's curiosity was clearly in evidence. He addressed the birds: "I heard you say, 'This must be the man. We should go and talk to him.' Whoever he is, call him and speak to him. I say this to you directly, without hesitation, since I'm afraid you may not put up with anyone interfering in your task by asking you who you are and where you're going. It's not that I'm not deeply gratified by the beauty of your presence. Just by looking at your shape, your movements, and your speech, anyone can see that you're no ordinary geese. You must be some godly species."

Sucimukhi answered with captivating sweetness, "Who else would we want to talk to here, son of Krishna? We went to Krishna at Indra's command, and he sent us on. We carry orders from both of them, and we were passing here on our way to somewhere else. We thought it wasn't right not to stop and pay our respects to you. It's always a mistake not to honor someone worthy of respect. What's more, your blessing is the very condition of our success in this mission. We are geese who play in the river of the gods. We're offspring of Kasyapa. Both Indra and your father treat us as their own and set us tasks accordingly. You are like Krishna's right hand; that's why we're telling you who we are. Remember us. Now give us leave to go."

Pradyumna said, "Maybe you shouldn't reveal your mission to anybody. That's fine. But tell me one thing. You said, 'This must be the man.' How did my name come up before? If you're allowed to talk about it, and if it doesn't delay you too much, stay a minute longer and tell me."

"It's true, it's a secret—all that you've asked. Also, we can't delay even for a moment. Still, in our eyes there's no difference between you and Krishna. So listen. We'll tell you what our task is and how your name came up."

But Sucimukhi was still hesitant, glancing this way and that way. Pradyumna followed her look with an expression of his own indicating a wish for privacy. His retinue understood and withdrew. Now, looking at him, the goose spoke in her uniquely mellifluous tone. "Listen. For a long time Krishna and Indra have been constantly planning how to kill the monster called Vajranabha. To be sure that he isn't planning to attack them first, they're sending us as spies to his city. That's where we're going now."

"Why would our elders waste so much thought, as if this were a big problem? When are they going to remember me? I could easily take care of it all by myself, if only they gave me the order. Probably they don't realize how strong we are, so they don't dare make the decision. All they need to do is to send me, and I'll kill the enemy who's troubling the gods."

Sucimukhi was suitably impressed. "Words fit for a hero! Only you could say that Indra and Krishna are wasting time deliberating, thinking this enemy could be very strong. Only you could say that if only they would stop being afraid and send you all by yourself, you would take care of the problem. It's only appropriate that someone like you would want to fight with that king of the antigods. A good hero is always excited when he finds someone who can stand up to him and give him a good fight, that isn't over too soon. Of course, real heroes won't just pick a fight for no reason. But if the right kind of battle should occur, they'll enter into it only too willingly.

WHEN WORDS FAIL

"But let that be. Let me tell you how your name was mentioned. We geese have been visiting Vajrapuri for some time. One day I happened to see the king's daughter, a stunning beauty, as she was playing near the palace pond. She was talking in private with her girlfriend. Even a female bird like me was completely overwhelmed by her infinite charm. What can I say?

What images can I conjure up
to describe the beauty of her body, from toe to tip?

Lotus blossoms, crescent moon, banyan fruits,
tortoise shell, a quiver of arrows, banana plants,
sandbanks, whirlpools, a lion's waist, golden pots,
fresh lotus stalks, leaf buds, the conch of the Love God,
jeweled mirrors, red coral, a sesame flower,
darting fish, a bow of horn, a piece of the moon,
the curves of the letter Sri, black bees[4]—

it's a shame we can't do better.

"Still, let me try again. Imagine the Love God holding high a bow, with tassles hanging on either side, and aiming an arrow at the sky. Now imagine a woman's face framed by the bow. The tip of the arrow is the dot on her forehead. Her eyebrows are the rounded curves of the bow, her nose coincides with the wrist of the archer, and the smile on her cheeks quivers like the tassles from the bow's two ends.

The black bees that we call her two eyes are fanatically devoted to her nose, which has defeated, once and for all, their inveterate enemy, the *campaka* flower.[5] That's why they happily dart back and forth, eager to serve. Or you might say that her eyes are like fish flashing through water in the direction of the two pools that are her ears; but since they can't decide which pool to choose, they're always caught in the middle, swimming madly in both directions.

The pearl in her nose ring is a condensed drop of Fame acquired when her lower lip came first in the beauty contests with red coral, fresh red buds, red *bimba* fruits, and the red *bandhujiva* flower.

Her perfect teeth that appear whenever she moves her lips to speak give you an impression of jasmine when the wind suddenly lifts the cover of the leaves. When she speaks, it's not only your ears that are happy. Your eyes are also bathed in a spray of white light bouncing off her teeth.

And I hope you wouldn't even dream of comparing her hands, like clusters of soft *gojjangi* flowers that open of their own accord, with the red lotus that has to be pried open at dawn by the sharp rays of the sun.

Her waist is visible only with reference to the dark hair in the middle. Otherwise, you might wonder whether it exists or not. Like a streak of lightning split down the middle in a monsoon cloud, you have to strain to see it.

In fact, her waist is teetering under the weight of her breasts and anything could happen at any moment. That's why Brahma has shored it up with folds of golden skin on her belly.

Those fussy logicians who argue that a flower growing in empty space emits no fragrance—and therefore does not exist—would be ashamed of themselves if they could see the golden flower of her belly button springing from her waist.

Without examining top and bottom carefully, poets often compare women's thighs to the golden banana stalk. But this doesn't work in her case. What's more, even if you turn the elephant's trunk upside down, it still is no better a metaphor for her soft, enticing thighs.

Her calves are like ripening rice in a well-watered field, which you can imagine as her anklets, and her knees could be turtles seeking a cool place in the water.

Even her toenails appear to be laughing at the conventions that compare her feet to lotuses and leaf buds.

Unlike someone who takes hold of the horn of a cow and gives a description of the whole cow, I have no way of truly describing her. So I've taken the easy path, like one who points out the star Arundhati, almost impossible to see, by pointing at a big star nearby.[6] All the images I've used are just a way of speaking. Each of her limbs is a thousand times beyond them.

What people say about beauty—that the God of Love made a mold in the shape of a woman and poured into it a mixture of brilliant moonlight, the soft texture of the lotus leaf, the sixteen shades of pure gold, and the streaking of lightning, just in order to produce someone like her—is simply and utterly inadequate.

I can try my best to describe her, but I can't touch
even a billionth of her beauty. Don't conclude from this
that I'm any less of a poet. I'm the best when it comes
to language. Speech herself trained me to be as eloquent
as she."

Now Sucimukhi revealed a bit of her biography: that she was the daughter of Sarandhara, one of the geese who pull Brahma's chariot, that because of that connection she was brought up by Sarasvati herself, in the inner chambers of the palace, and that through the kindness of the goddess she had learned all skills and had them at her fingertips. The goddess gave her the name Sucimukhi, "Perfect Speech."

"One day Sarasvati set up a poetry contest between me and her pet parrot. When she acknowledged that I had the edge, she praised me and combed my feathers with her fingernails. She looked at me with affection, curiosity, kindness, and warmth and bestowed a title on me: 'Mother of Similes and Hyperbole.' She even had it inscribed on an anklet, which she tied on my foot with her own hands. If you want, just take a look." And Sucimukhi showed off the anklet, turning it around so Pradyumna could read the letters. "Still, even for me, accomplished as I am, that girl's beauty is beyond words. You might suggest that I try to paint her likeness and show it to you. But to paint any one part of her body, you first have to contemplate it; and the moment you think about it, your mind is lost in her beauty; but then there's no way to paint with a distracted mind.

What's more, if it were possible for a person to replicate her in painting, this implies that the Creator God—for example—could have created some other woman like her, somewhere else. But Brahma himself once admitted, in my presence, that he didn't create her. It was the First Goddess, Parvati, who made her with her miraculous artistic skill.[7]

I knew this, but it had receded into the depths of my consciousness until we were speaking just now. It's well known that experiences resurface in the course of conversation.

I heard Brahma say the girl was born to Vajranabha's wife through a burst of Parvati's creative energy. Later I started wondering why her physical beauty is so far beyond anything in this world. Then I understood that these two matters are connected, since I remembered what I'd forgotten—that is, what Brahma had said.[8]

Incidentally, her name is Prabhavati, 'Luminous,' and this name is not without meaning. You yourself are the full moon rising out of the vast ocean of the Yadu family. I saw Prabhavati show her friend a painting that, according to her, the goddess herself had painted and given her in a dream. Because I, too, saw that picture, when I saw you now I realized you were exactly like that image. That's when I said, 'This must be the man.'

But I've got to go. I can't delay. Good-bye. Please give me leave to go." With this, the goose and her entourage flew up into the sky. They flew in formation, so fast that they looked like a wire stretched across the sky, without gap or break, and the golden radiance of their wings seemed to be carrying the power of Pradyumna all the way to the demon's city. It was as if they were the visible forms of his dazzling fame. Holding their wings still, stretched to the limit, they formed a two-pronged line, as if to swallow up the sky. They seemed to be challenging the clouds on either side to compete with them in whiteness as they flapped their wings in unison and showed off their aeronautical skills, flying up, down, sideways. They painted the sky white, as if sandalpaste had been sprinkled all through it. The gilded tips of their wings seemed to trace threshold designs in space. Then they arranged themselves in military order, wing to wing; when you looked through the spaces between goose and goose, you could imagine the dark Yamuna River, daughter of the Sun, flowing into the white Ganges of the sky. Keeping together, they reached Vajrapuri and, as many times before, came down for a landing in its ponds and pools.

Sucimukhi chose the pool of the inner palace. The girls were playing in the water, and Sucimukhi made herself come close to them without fear. She put up with the spray from their splashing, and she steeled her nerves to withstand their sudden cries. She struggled to catch a whiff of the stamens from the play lotuses they held in their hands. Little by little, she got used to the girls and was able to stay close to them.

PRADYUMNA'S MEDITATION

Meanwhile, Pradyumna was meditating on ultimate truth, that is, on Prabhavati's beauty. He trained his mind to follow the path of the Upanishad in its definitive form, that is, the revealing words of the Goose who Spoke Truth. The more he concentrated, the more attractive this truth became. He did not notice people standing right beside him; or if he noticed them, he had no idea how to behave with them. He heard nothing of what was said to him, unless it was repeated many times; or if he did hear, he would ask, "What was that you said?" He hardly moved unless prodded to go take a bath, and so on; and even then, he would do everything upside down. He asked for nothing from his servants; or if he did ask, he would make confused and disconnected demands. He was unable to divert his mind from the unique and stunning vision of Prabhavati that could be clearly seen in the mirror of the goose's words.

With rising desire, following the words of the goose,
he intensified the beauty of the images she had used,
like "bees" or "moon," a thousand times over.
*   He composed the girl*
in his mind out of hair, face, and all the limbs of her body

as far as he could imagine. Finally, he got a glimpse of her
in his inner eye.

In this way he went on without pause
connecting each of the images to the proper part
of her perfect body and magnifying the beauty of the similes
a thousand times over, to the limit thought
could reach. He saw her exactly
as she was. There is nothing beyond the grasp
of an unfettered mind.

Once he'd seen her, he took her into himself
over and over, thinking none was like her.
Then he really wanted to meet her, and wanting this,
he despaired: "How could I ever be so lucky?"
In despair, he sighed deeply, despising life
without her. He tried to think of ways
to go to her, and finding none, he lost hope.
Helpless, he let his mind run riot in fantasy,
but as there was no end to the fantasy, he sank
into grief. In his grief, if anyone tried even to talk to him,
he'd be angry—for he could not bear this separation.

><><><

Intelligent, courageous, tactful, modest, a good strategist—
such was my father. He garlanded space itself with his fame.

><><><

This is the second chapter in the book called *Prabhavati-pradyumnamu*, composed by Suraya, son of Pingali Amaranarya. All great scholars celebrate his poetry and sing of his modesty.

Chapter Three

*Pingali Amaramatya always meditated
on the meaning of Siva's stories.
In fame he was like a second sun.*

PRADYUMNA SENDS A LETTER

One day Pradyumna was sitting alone with his cheek resting on his hand, and he was thinking:

*"Will my eyes ever be fortunate enough to see her?
They say even entering that city
is no small thing. Let's imagine I do manage
to get in, how can I not embrace her?
But how can this embrace take place
unless she wants it, too?*

*Still, there's one thing Sucimukhi said
that gives me hope. She said that stunning girl
was staring at a picture of someone
who looks like me. But can I rely
on those words? There are always people
who look like other people.*

*I should have asked her for more details.
Instead, I hid my desire and put on a mask
of pseudodignity. This stupid shyness
froze my lips. The goose may have thought
that I didn't care. She didn't stay even for a second.
People with any self-respect don't waste words
on those who show no interest.*

If only I'd revealed at least a little of what was in my mind, the goose would have pressed me to express my feelings for that girl—and would have said something more. Or so it seems to me now. Otherwise, she wouldn't have taken the time to describe her so elaborately. On the other hand, you have to consider the possibility that certain people with an artistic feel for words simply can't stop when, on occasion, they begin to describe some absolutely amazing object. In that case, the long description may have nothing to do with me.

"The goose came down to inform me of the mission on which Krishna and Indra had sent her—simply to watch my reaction. Possibly they're thinking of sending me against the monster. That's why she said to me that I'm Krishna's right-hand man.

"So all in all, putting it all together and thinking it through, the balance comes down on the hopeful side. If you think along these lines, it's quite certain that the portrait Prabhavati has is really mine. And if you ask who could possibly have painted me so accurately, the answer is: Parvati. It all fits.

If you assume Parvati painted the picture and gave
    it to Prabhavati,
could she have had some other reason? She could not.
You don't show a painting to a young girl in a palace
unless you're revealing her future husband.
But maybe it was only one picture out of a series of many
potential husbands, and I might fail the final selection!
No. The goose said the goddess herself
gave the picture to the girl, with her blessings,
and the girl was looking at it intently.
But maybe Parvati wouldn't want this marriage to happen.
No. She does. Prabhavati is her own daughter.
Maybe it's all one big game?
That's unlikely. The goose said Brahma himself
corroborated her story.

Brahma told the goose that he was not the creator of Prabhavati, and the goose told me, but I didn't think to ask more—maybe Brahma knew who was going to be the girl's husband, for example. But what's the point of blaming myself now? There were many opportunities for me to ask questions while the goose was going on and on, and still I didn't say a word. If the bird concluded that I'm not interested and, as a result, fails even to mention me to Prabhavati when an occasion arises, what can I do now?

"Will she go at least one more time to Prabhavati? Maybe not, since she has nothing interesting to report about me. Or maybe she will, if she thinks Prabhavati has something to do with the gods' mission. There's at least a chance she'll go to see her again. After all, that goose is an intelligent bird. She may have seen into my heart. She probably knows the proverb 'Not saying no is like saying yes.'

"For that matter, even if she has no business with Prabhavati, she'll still pay her a visit. How can she not? Anyone who sees her can't help wanting to see her again."

Pradyumna, lost in these thoughts, had created Prabhavati's full presence in his imagination. Now he rushed to embrace her with true passion and, not finding her in his arms, he was shaken. Since time weighed heavily, he went into his garden. But the garden was full of Prabhavati. Thick clusters of flowers had the fullness of her breasts. Tender red leaf buds told him of her hands. Vines hanging from the trees whispered the delicacy of her arms. Bees darting from flower to flower were the swift glances of her eyes. Every white flower evoked her smile, and all her loveliness flowed in honey.

He had gone out in the hope of forgetting his distress, but in fact he forgot everything but his distress. It was a good illustration of what people say, "You hope for one thing and what you get is the exact opposite."

He went from vine to vine, thinking each one was Prabhavati. "This must be her hand," he would say hopefully, and then drop it in disappointment: "It's only a leaf." Then, "Here are her breasts"—but no, they were only clusters of flowers. "I've found her sari"—alas, only a dust of pollen. Driven by desire, he reached for her dark braid and found a swarm of bees instead. "I'll never find her, ingrate that I am. The bird came to me out of the goodness of her heart, to do me a favor, and I didn't open my heart to her. Forget about meeting the girl. If I could just see that goose one more time, I'd consider myself lucky. Will she come just to give me news of that monster, Vajranabha? And if she comes, will she come close enough to tell me if Prabhavati is well?

"I fell in love just by hearing about this girl, and now I'm in pain. But she actually saw a picture of me with her own eyes. She must be suffering even more. I've heard that falling in love from seeing a picture can be a serious business. What is worse, when the goose tells her how she spoke with me but I said nothing in return, the girl may give up on me.

"Who knows when the goose will come back, if at all, after completing her mission? Who knows when I'll be able to tell her my feelings and send her to Prabhavati? I think I'll write her a letter right now, with a message to be delivered to Prabhavati." So he wrote out a letter addressed to Sucimukhi. Then he wondered who could deliver the letter. He returned to the garden[1] and, in the urgency of his desire, called out to whatever was flying north, without stopping to think whether they could carry a message or not.

"You parrots! Kindly tell me. Are you by any chance
heading to Vajrapuri?
What about you bees? Are you by any chance
heading to Vajrapuri?
Speak to me, cuckoos—are you by any chance
heading to Vajrapuri?
Winds from the Malaya Hills, are you by any chance
heading to Vajrapuri?
Stop for a moment and answer me, white clouds and
*   regal geese.*
Are you by any chance heading to Vajrapuri?"

As he was crying out like this, a certain parrot flying through the sky heard the distress in his voice and took pity on him. "Yes, I'm going to Vajrapuri," the parrot said. "What can I do for you? Tell me in one or two words."

"Great bird, a certain royal goose called Sucimukhi is in that city. Find out where she lives and deliver this letter to her. That's my request."

"I'll do you this favor," said the parrot, "but I must fly. There's no time to talk. Just tie the letter under my wings, where no one can see it. Hurry." She came down close to him, and he quickly did as she said. She flew off without further delay.

THE GOOSE GOES TO THE PALACE

By that time, Sucimukhi and her retinue had already moved into the inner part of the palace, near the women. She was patiently awaiting the right moment to make friends with Prabhavati. One day

Prabhavati came with her friend Ragavallari to the garden near the pond in the hope of cooling the fierce heat of her lovesickness.

Enhanced by her smiles, jasmine took on an added whiteness.
The bees became darker by copying her eyes.
Fresh leaf buds glowed at the touch of her hands.
The winds from the south compounded their fragrance with her hot
    sighs.
Then all of them in turn heightened her pain.
That's what happens. If you help someone who is weak, fickle, or unsta-
    ble,
they hurt you in the end.

She was met by a depressing landscape, all too like a battle-ground. Red leaf buds seemed to her to be spears soaked in the blood of lonely lovers. Flowers flowing with honey were lamps lit with the fat of lovers who had died from longing. Bees were dashing from flower to flower like dark bullets shot from Love's musket. Pollen spilling from the blossoms was dust stirred up by Love's army on the march. And listening to the calls of the parrots and the cuckoos, she could hear bards singing of Love and his devastating victories.

Feeling much worse, Prabhavati said to Ragavallari, "This is no way to spend time. It's making everything harder. I've had enough of this garden. I need to see my lover's face again. The goddess will take care of me. Bring the picture. Fast."

When the picture arrived, she looked at it and saw the young man in all his captivating gestures and movements, as if emerging from her own determination to behold him, out of the depths of her own feelings.[2] She stared at it head-on, then from an angle, her eyes wide open, then half closed, her shifting moods overwhelming her as she watched.

"I thought I'd be satisfied just by seeing it, but the longer I look, the more excited I become. It's something new every moment. He won't let me take my eyes away. I can't stand it." Overcome, she rushed at the painting and embraced it.

For a few moments she was still, her eyes half closed in a kind of ecstasy. Then her mind took over and told her it was only a picture. She placed it at a distance and looked again. "If there were such a man somewhere in the world, and if I could really embrace him, and if he, for all my shyness, would stay with me and do whatever he felt like doing, then, and only then, life would be worth living."

Her mind was boiling over in restlessness and despair. The distance was unbearable. "I must not have served the goddess well. There was something wrong somewhere—with me, with the ritual, or with the way I performed it. Otherwise she wouldn't punish me like this. Is there really a man like this somewhere in the world? If he existed, word would have gotten round that he's here or there or somewhere. It's all a trick by the goddess."

Sucimukhi, who was waiting nearby, heard of all of this and thought to herself, "This is the right moment for me to make her my fast friend." Thinking out a strategy, she sauntered slowly by, as if by chance, right in front of Prabhavati, and seemed to examine the picture herself, very carefully, again and again, in a strange kind of way. Prabhavati took notice, smiled, and said to her friend, "Look at this weird bird. Does it know something? It keeps staring at the painting."

Now the goose said sweetly, "Listen, young lady. You're right. Birds like us don't know anything. But let me tell you why I'm looking so attentively at the picture in your hand. Once, in a certain place, I saw a man. I haven't found anyone like him anywhere. Suddenly, I see his likeness in this picture. I was just wondering whether someone who knew him had painted this picture or, if not, whether there's another man like him somewhere or other."

Prabhavati was flooded by amazement, joy, doubt. Looking straight at the goose, she said, "What did you say? Tell me again. Did you say you saw a man exactly like this one? Or is there some slight difference? Come take a closer look. Listening to the way you use language, I think you must be a great mind. So you know what I'm feeling, don't you? You have nothing to fear."

Said the goose, "I know there's no reason to be afraid. I can tell just by looking who causes harm and who doesn't. But I'm not so rude as to barge into a private conversation without being invited."

The two women were surprised; they looked at one another and smiled. They delighted in the incongruously mature speech of this talking goose; in fact, they were completely won over and wanted to hear more and more. Ragavallari said, "Have you ever heard or seen any human being talking with such evident experience?" Then, looking at the bird affectionately and happily: "What you said is right. But the two of us were actually not talking about anything very private. We had a certain doubt, which perhaps you can resolve for us. You said you've seen a certain man. Come here and take a close look. Tell us definitively if the one you saw and the one in the painting are really and truly the same. This young woman and I have made a wager as to whether a man like the painting does or does not exist."

"What do I care if you're asking this question to settle a bet or for some other reason? In any case, I'll tell you what you want to hear."

The women exchanged glances. "This bird knows more than meets the eye." Meanwhile, the goose came close, pretending to take a very careful look at the painting, and said, "This picture is that man. There's simply no room for doubt."

Ragavallari ran forward and picked up the bird in a burst of excitement. Tenderly she stroked her feathers and put her down next to Prabhavati. "You're no goose. You're the goddess of our good fortune who has taken this shape. You helped me win my bet. This silly girl is constantly annoying me by denying that such a handsome man can exist in any conceivable world."

Prabhavati said to her friend, "Not so fast, Ragavallari. To settle the matter once and for all, we still need to know just what particular qualities of that man are in this picture."

The goose pointed at the painting. "Just look. Here are the scars on his chest from the time he killed Sambara, the enemy of the gods. And here you can see, on his neck, the marks of his wife Rati's bracelets.[3] I wonder who knew him so well, this hero in war and love, that he could paint him so true to life. From what I've said so far, you must have guessed his name and his family. They're very famous. On the other hand, you're closeted in that palace, so perhaps you don't know. I'd tell you but

it's best to answer only to the extent
you've been invited to speak. That's what
people say. To settle your bet
what I've said should be enough.
No more words.

You're Prabhavati, aren't you? I've heard of you before. And this woman is Ragavallari. I heard you calling her by that name. Don't forget me. Good-bye."

She was about to fly off into the sky, but Prabhavati held her firmly in her two hands and pleaded with her, in a thousand ways, to stay. "Watching your wings white as moonlight is a whole festival. To see the golden streaks at the edge of your wings is another kind of happiness. The way you walk with such dignity is a joy in itself. There's no greater treat than to savor your delicious words. You make me want more of you. We've hardly begun to know one another. I can't lose you now. From now on, Ragavallari is my friend only in name. You're the real thing. I'm begging you to be my friend. You simply have to say yes."

"You may like me now; you've described me so beautifully. But when you notice that I'm intruding on your secrets, you'll want to get rid of me. So don't let me invade your privacy. Give me leave to go."

Now Ragavallari intervened. "Why do you keep torturing us by saying you want to go? You're no obstacle to our private matter. Quite the contrary, you'll be a help. That's why we want to be friends, not just because you're so charming. Listening to your words, we have the feeling that you know what we mean. But because we're palace women, we're not in a position to tell you about that matter openly. Still, you made it clear right from the beginning that you wouldn't do anything without being asked directly. So there's no point in talking under cover. It's like trying to put a drum to sleep by patting on it. We can't compete with you in words. That handsome man you saw is the one hope for this woman. Tell us, please, about his name and family. If you delay, you'll be putting her life in danger. Speak at once. Save her. Afterward I'll tell you about us."

Sucimukhi put aside her oblique manner of speaking and said straight out, "You live in a palace, and you're not used to speaking plainly about your inner thoughts. I had to interpret things for myself. So how, under these conditions, could I speak about a young man in your presence? That's why I hesitated. Now that you've spoken out, I'll tell you."

She looked at Prabhavati. "Here's the story of the man who stole your heart. In the Bharata land, there's a city called Dvaraka. Not even the Creator can describe it to the end, for its splendor has no end. If I were to attempt to describe it to you to the best of my ability, even a little, you'd find it would distract you from the main story. So let it go."

They giggled. "You're right about that. You're obviously a good storyteller."

"Krishna, who is Vishnu born in a human family, lives in that city. Among his sixteen thousand wives, there are eight whom he really adores. Among them, one named Rukmini is number one. She has a son called Pradyumna. That's him in the picture. He's courage itself. The very epitome of strength. Noble, glowing with beauty and generosity. But why go on heaping up words? His virtues are exactly what his beauty requires."

Happiness was exploding
all over Prabhavati, sweeping all
before it. She couldn't hold it in.
It came out visibly in her face though
she was trying her best, in all modesty
and shyness, to contain it.

Ragavallari was regarding her with no less joy. "This proves what the goddess who gave you the picture said. You heard his name and family, and now you know for certain where he lives, thanks to this fine goose. You can stop worrying now. Listen to how she speaks. She must have grown up among famous scholars and artists. She has a prize anklet as a trophy on her foot." And she read off, to her amazement, the letters inscribed on the anklet—the bird's title. Then she heard the goose tell the story of her birth and education.

"She's the only one we can depend on for help," said Ragavallari to her friend. "There's no one else." And she related to the goose all that Prabhavati had suffered, all the stages of her lovesickness. "See for yourself how she looks," she said.

"The nose ring she wears is not a blue sapphire. It's a white pearl dark-
*   ened by her burning sighs.*
What she has on her upper arms are not armlets but rings that measure
*   how thin she has grown.*
That black mark on her breasts is not musk but mascara that's dripped
*   down from her eyes.*
Her earrings are not diamonds but rather rubies reflecting the extreme
*   pallor of her cheeks.*

As you see, my good bird, her life is in your hands.

"There are secrets you can't share with your mother, your sisters, or any other close relative. Such are the feelings that come when you're overwhelmed by love, which can be shared only by the closest of friends. Even if you give your life for such a friend, your debt remains unpaid.

"You know what a good friend should do. The wise say you become friends if you share seven words or take seven steps together. So go quickly to that young prince of the Yadu family and tell him how beautiful this woman is. Touch his heart. Find a way to fulfil her wishes."

Said the goose, "I've already had occasion to describe to him the beauty of each and every limb of this girl. Do you want to know when that was? Listen. I had already seen her great loveliness before. When recently I saw him, I thought at once that these two would be a perfect pair. So I took the opportunity to speak to him about her. He listened in silence, saying neither yes nor no. I left it at that, since I knew nothing about you."

Prabhavati paled. The goose comforted her, "Don't worry. The matter need not end here. There are things we can do. Since he said nothing when I described you, I can't promise that I can bring him to you. On the other hand, I'll happily present you with any young man you fancy from among the Siddhas or Gandharvas or gods or antigods.

And don't worry that the goddess Parvati
won't approve if you choose some man other
than the one she chose for you. She always
gives in to her devotees. She wants
whatever you want.

In my opinion, you should forget about Pradyumna. Anyway, it's doubtful if you can get him. Just tell me which one of the gods or antigods or Siddhas or Vidyadharas or Gandharvas you'd like, and I'll show him one-thousandth part of your beauty. That will be more than enough to set him on fire, like the chants priests use to ignite a sacrificial rite. I'll make him your slave. You underestimate the power of your beauty. Is there any man in the world who would be immune to your charms? Maybe there's one, that prince of the Yadu family who is, perhaps, blinded by his own incomparable handsomeness. Leave him alone. I roam through all the worlds and I see all kinds of captivating young men. I can't say they're his equals, but if you like, I can paint their images and show you. Just choose the one you want."

Prabhavati turned a deaf ear to these words. She mused for a moment and said, sadly, "You've described the man I've been in love with for a long, long time. Don't torture me now with these sour words. Up till now I've trusted your good taste. My father Vajranabha has already done what you suggested. He showed me pictures of gods and Gandharvas and Siddhas and Yaksas and Vidyadharas and antigods and gave me the freedom to choose any one I liked. I didn't even feel like taking a second look at any of them, not to speak of wanting one. Let fate take its course.

"My father never showed me a picture of this man. Maybe there were no painters equal to the task. Or maybe he didn't know about him. Maybe it was because he's only a human being—or because he belongs to the enemy clan. I hear that Krishna is bent on destroying the gods' enemies.

"But is it worth worrying about that? You have heard how I feel about that man and also what the goddess said to me, and still you expect me to agree to choose someone else? Obviously, you haven't seen into the depths of my heart. Let me tell you something.

"You can forget about my taking any man other than Prad-yumna. I've taken a vow. If that noble man doesn't want me, I'll burn myself to death in the flames of love and move on to my next life. In fact, it looks like this second option is the only one I have. You know why? It's not only that he said nothing when you told him about me. You also mentioned a certain woman who left bracelet marks on his neck. Apparently, I didn't pray for him the way she did in her previous life."

Prabhavati thought for a moment, envious of her rival's good luck. "Don't you wish you were *her* hands?" she said, looking at her hands. "You'd be embracing him this very minute."

She turned to her breasts: "If you were only *her* breasts, you'd be pressed against his chest."

Then to her cheeks: "If you were *her* cheeks, you'd enjoy his kisses."

Finally, to her ears: "If you were *her* ears, you could hear his pillow talk."

Summing up, with pity: "All of you got stuck with me. The fortune-tellers who read my fate from my body when I was young got it all wrong."

She went on like this for quite some time, in the usual agonies of separation, before turning to Sucimukhi with a question: "Goose, there's one last thing I want to ask you. Tell me how you feel. Don't lie to me. You're my dearest friend. Do you think it's a good idea for you to go one more time to see Pradyumna, to tell him of my distress, in the hopes that he might become my friend? Or is it not? I'm being strangled by this impossible hope. It stops the breath inside my body and fans the fire of my desire. It's getting worse minute by minute. Go find out one way or the other, put an end to this unendurable suspense. You'll be saving my life."

The goose knew that no one could discourage this woman from wanting Krishna's son, and that if something was not done quickly to help her, some disaster would ensue. So she said, "I was just testing the strength of your passion. Trust me. I'll bring your husband to you. I don't know why he didn't respond at that time; probably he was not fully attentive. But now you'll see. As soon as he hears of your extraordinary birth and beauty, he's sure to fall in love and start suffering. In fact, it's all destiny. I'll explain.

"Once Brahma and Sarasvati had a lovers' quarrel. Brahma couldn't bear the tension, so he looked for some dependable messenger he could send to his wife. He found me—since at that time I was a very close adviser and playmate of Sarasvati's. He summoned me and gave me a message for her.

'The Vedas live on my tongue because of your lucid presence.
All the fragrance of poetry and music emerges from your play.
The melodies of vina and flute embody your love.
The whole world is in business because you allow it to happen.
If you're upset even a little, I have no joy left in life.
How you can stay angry for so long at your willing slave?

Go recite this to Sarasvati, tell her how I blame her for everything.' Writhing in love, he then turned to the God of Desire and said, 'Lord of love, why do you keep hurting me like this? What do you gain from it? You are going to suffer just like me very soon—in terrible longing for a woman named Prabhavati. Don't be so sure of yourself.'

"When I heard that, I had to ask. 'This woman you're talking about, is she more beautiful than Rati, if she can attract Love's attention away from his wife?'

"Brahma replied, 'There's no comparison. Those who know can tell you that Prabhavati is easily three to four times more beautiful than Rati. You'll never find anybody that I've created who is as lovely as Prabhavati. Parvati made her.'

"He urged me to rush to appease Sarasvati. I knew how impatient he was, so I didn't stay to ask any further questions.

After some time, I came to know that you are that Prabhavati. I think it's clear from all this that your husband, Krishna's son, will find separation from you even more unbearable than you find it to be from him. None of Rati's exquisite charms can stop him. Have no doubt."

Still, there was a question in Prabhavati's mind. She looked at Ragavallari, who addressed the goose. "You're trying to console her, but the story you told doesn't add up. Your words are very strange. So what if Kama, the God of Desire, falls in love with Prabhavati? How does that make the man she wants fall in love with her?"

The goose smiled. "You know who Kama is. That model of maleness has been reborn, even more handsome than before, if that's possible, as Rukmini's son. He's Pradyumna."

So now the goose had laid to rest all doubts and questions. She was still there as Prabhavati began to speak, all aflame. "Even if what you say is true, who knows how far away that city is? How long will it take you to get there? And if you reach it, when will you find the right moment to see him, to tell him what I'm feeling? And when you tell him, how can he show me his love freely? And even if he shows me love, under what pretext can we get my father to let him into the city? Vajranabha is very suspicious. Since when does he care about my wishes? How can I get across this vast ocean of wanting? It's all a hopeless hope."

In her despair, the bright red of her lips had seeped into her eyes.

A LOVE LETTER

At that juncture, she caught side of a parrot flapping its wings in terror, as it was caught in a noose hanging from a nearby tree. She got up quickly and, with her friend and the goose in tow, rushed to help. She took the parrot gently in her hands as she disentangled its feet from the noose. The bird shook itself free from her grip and flew up into the sky. In the flurry of her flight, a letter slipped out from under her wings. Prabhavati turned to the goose. "Did you see that? Let's look into it. I wonder who's sending letters to whom? Can you bring the parrot back?"

"Of course. How far can she go?" said the goose, racing off after the parrot.

Prabhavati looked at her friend. "Who could have put this noose in my garden in the first place? It's very odd."

Said Ragavallari to her friend, who was staring with eyes wide as the lotus as it opens at dawn, "It's my fault. Please forgive me. I set it up as a trap for the cuckoos who were driving you crazy with their singing. What's really strange is this letter. Let's see what it says."

She opened it and began to read in a clear voice: "'Greetings to Sucimukhi, who bears the honorable title "Mother of Similes and Hyperbole" graciously bestowed by the goddess Sarasvati and inscribed on an anklet on her foot. This is a secret letter written by Pradyumna, driven by love. You spoke to me about Pra-Pra-bhavati . . .'"

Ragavallari jumped up and down in excitement, waving her arms. "Listen," she cried, "this is a letter sent by your lover to you! What luck!"

"Is that really what the letter says, or are you just teasing me? Show me the letter." She stretched out her hand. Ragavallari ran a few paces, trying to escape her, clutching the letter. "I swear by God, that's how it is. Let me read it through for you. You can see it afterward."

"You're lying to me. It can't be me. Who knows who that Pra-Pra-bhavati is? Look carefully at the letter. You don't have to give it to me."

"As if you didn't know it's your name. He was so excited that he wrote the first syllable twice."

"Well—if you say so . . . Anyway, read the rest. Stop running around. I'll keep quiet."

"In that case—listen." She went on reading from where she had stopped. "'You spoke to me about Pra-Pra-bhavati. If I didn't say anything at the time, it's because I was pretending to be proud. But you described her so graphically that each of her features has been imprinted on my mind and has acquired a life of its own, as if carved in my heart. I can hardly bear such beauty. I'm exhausted by the weight of it. Dear goose, beg her to revive me with a kiss.'"

At this point, Prabhavati snatched the letter from her hands.

Ragavallari let it go without further struggle. "It's not right for me to read further, anyway," she said. "He may have written out his love in very intimate words.[4] Save it for when you're alone."

Prabhavati, feeling a mixture of anger and embarrassment, wanted to crumple the letter in her hands. Ragavallari invoked all the gods to keep her from doing this. "Stop being such a child. Enough of this foolishness. Give it to me. Or if you won't give it to me, at least take good care of it. Anyway, it's not your letter. That splendid young man wrote it to Sucimukhi. How can we destroy it before she's had a chance to look at it? What kind of friendship is that? Think it over. Don't be so stupid. When a lover sends a love letter, a woman lucky enough to receive it treasures it like a gift from god. It's bad luck to treat it casually." She threatened and cajoled and admonished Prabhavati in this way, barely stopping her from destroying the letter.

Goose and Parrot

Meanwhile the goose had caught up with the parrot in the sky and grabbed it tightly with her feet. The parrot twisted and turned, screamed, bit the goose's feet, and in general caused a lot of trouble. The goose was enraged. "You smart-aleck bird, don't get yourself killed. Come quietly with me. For whom are you bearing messages, and what kind of letters are they, anyway? The king's daughter is standing there waiting for me to bring you to her."

"Kill me if you like, just don't bring me to her. If you kill me, only *I* will die. If you take me there, you never know what might happen to many others."

"Whether I let you go or take you there doesn't matter. We've got the letter. But if you drag your feet, you're the one who will suffer. If you come quietly, I'll speak well of you to Prabhavati and see that you're released." Sucimukhi dragged her along.

The parrot said, "Why so adamant? If you ask me, I'll tell you my secret—as a friend. You're no fool. You'll gain nothing by torturing me. If I hold out and don't talk, there's still hope that my mission will be fulfilled. If I give in and reveal it under pressure, I gain nothing, the mission fails, and I still get the pain. So take me to some secluded spot and listen. If you think what I have done was wrong, you can decide then what to do with me."

The goose agreed. She took the parrot to a hillock where there were no trees or other plants. Still pinning down the parrot's wings, the goose demanded to hear the whole story of the letter.

The parrot said, "I went to Dvaraka on some business. As I was returning, I saw an extraordinarily handsome young man looking very disturbed in a garden. He was calling out,

"You parrots! Kindly tell me. Are you by any chance
heading to Vajrapuri?
What about you bees? Are you by any chance
heading to Vajrapuri?
Speak to me, cuckoos—are you by any chance
heading to Vajrapuri?
Winds from the Malaya Hills, are you by any chance
heading to Vajrapuri?
Stop for a moment and answer me, you clouds and regal geese.
Are you by any chance heading to Vajrapuri?"

He was calling to whomever he happened to see. I felt sorry for him and said, "I'm going to Vajrapuri. What can I do for you?"

⊳—+•◦▸—0—◂•+—◅

He followed the Vedic path as prescribed in the revealed and
**   remembered texts.**
In diplomacy, he was more skillful than Sukra, the advisor to the
**   antigods.**
He had self-control, courage, patience, and great dignity.
Such was my father.

⊳—+•◦▸—0—◂•+—◅

This is the third chapter in the book called *Prabhavati-pradyumnamu*, composed by Suraya, son of Pingali Amaranarya. All great scholars celebrate his poetry and sing of his modesty.

Chapter Four

Amaranarya, in all his brilliance, blessed by the goddess Sri, wise as Brhaspati—the guru of the gods—always enjoyed the company of poets and delighted in their poems.

THE GOOSE INTERROGATES THE PARROT

The parrot continued: "The prince in the garden looked at me and said, 'Great bird, a certain royal goose called Sucimukhi is in that city. Please find out where she lives and deliver this letter to her. That's my request.' I was deeply moved by his distress and, out of kindness, without thinking much about the consequences, I agreed to take the letter. I thought to myself, 'What harm is there in delivering a letter to a goose?' I asked him to tie the letter tightly inside my wings. When I came to this garden, I heard the cackling of geese in the ponds and saw you in the company of those girls. I was just resting in a tree and wondering if Sucimukhi could be there when I got caught in the noose. That's when my troubles began."

The goose was very happy to hear this statement, which suited her purpose well. "That's as much as she knows," Sucimukhi concluded and, hiding her joy, decided to play down the importance of the letter, to distract the parrot with other matters, and to let her go. "Anyone who writes a letter addressed to a bird must be out of his mind," she said. "There's no point in pressing you for more details. Just tell me without lying: Why did you have to go to Dvaraka in the first place?"

The parrot hesitated, saying nothing. The goose pressed her further, thinking perhaps there was something of interest here, yet the parrot stood her ground fearlessly. "I prefer to die. I won't say anything until you take a vow to keep the secret. Strong people will never reveal their masters' secrets, not even if you give them all the money in the world or hold a knife to their neck."

So the goose took the vow. Now the parrot could tell the story. "Vajranabha has a brother, a fierce king named Sunabha. He has two charming daughters, Gunavati and Candravati. One day Narada happened to go to his court. Sunabha received him with honor and sent him with the palace guards into the inner chambers, where the queens and daughters bowed to him, to receive his blessing. Narada, pleased with their devotion, blessed the girls: 'You'll find loving husbands and give birth to sons.' The maidservants wanted to know more. 'Who exactly will their husbands be? Tell us that, too.'

"Narada thought for a minute and said, 'These two young women will marry two very handsome young men from Dvaraka, Gada and Samba, born in the Yadu clan.' This upset them. 'Everything was just fine until we asked this question. Dvaraka is far away, and who are these two men, Gada and Samba, anyway? If the king finds out, it will be a disaster. Dvaraka is an enemy city.' They hushed up what Narada had said, so no one could know. But the two girls, from that moment on, were totally devoted in their hearts to their husbands, Gada and Samba. They prayed and performed rites for their welfare.

"Meanwhile, as they grew up, their desire to be with their husbands deepened. Since there was no word from distant Dvaraka, they grew weak and thin, though their beauty was still striking. I'm a close friend of theirs. They brought me up and taught me to talk. They treated me as one of them. I've been longing to do something to repay the immense kindness they showed me. So I said to them, 'Girls, I'll go find out how your husbands are and report back to you. Trust me. If possible, I'll speak to them in secret and make your desire known to them. I'll bring back word. Don't worry, give me leave to go.'

"They, however, were reluctant to let me go. They didn't want to be without me. Still, I made them consent and took off for Dvaraka city, where I accomplished whatever I could. As I was returning, this letter fell to my lot. You know all the rest. I'm afraid that if Prabhavati sees me and marks me, some danger might befall Candravati and Gunavati. Today is the day I mentioned as the very latest I would return. They must be anxiously waiting for me. I should see them. Let me go.

As cataka birds wait for raindrops
and cakora birds for the moon
and the lotus for the sun,
they are waiting for me."

Said the goose, "I'll follow you. I won't leave you yet. If you call those girls and prove to me that everything you said is true, then I'll let you go and also let them know that I could be their friend."

"Fine," said the parrot and flew off, with the goose closely following. After ascertaining that no one else was present, she entered the inner palace. Taking cover beside an alcove where pigeons nest,[1] she looked to see there were no other women around before she called to those two girls.

"That's the voice of our parrot!" they cried, feeling their weariness dispelled as if by a touch of cooling camphor. They came close and saw the goose covering the parrot—and went white. To reassure them, the parrot spoke, "There's nothing to worry about. This bird promised me that she would only help me and those who sent me, and that she would never cause harm." She went on to tell them how she had met the goose, and she reassured them: this goose would keep their secret.

Sucimukhi, moved by the girls' respect, released the parrot. Now the parrot turned to each of the girls and said, by turns, "Let me tell you about my mission. Candravati, your husband Gada, a second Indra, is healthy and well in Dvaraka. Gunavati, your beloved Samba, a solid mass of virtue, is also there, happy and hearty. I made friends with both of them and met with each of them separately at the right moment, without the other's knowledge. I told them all about your love. I told them you won't survive if they ignore you. These men are ready to take you, by one means or another. They said that if the two of you should lose courage and die, you'll bear the burden of two sins—suicide and mariticide."

The girls covered their ears with their hands. "God forbid! Don't utter those heavy words. May they live long lives. The word they spoke will be the raft that keeps us afloat on this ocean of separation. Until such time as they think up a way of saving us, we won't do anything hasty."

The goose intervened. "I'll find a way to bring your husbands here quite quickly. Don't forget me and my friendship. I found this parrot because I'm a close friend of Prabhavati's; now I know you, too. But I shouldn't stay any longer. Good-bye for now. I'll take care that this secret of yours doesn't leak out; I'll invent something and cover it up. Rest assured." With this, she took her leave of the two girls, whose hearts, she could see, were content.

THE GOOSE REPORTS TO PRABHAVATI

She returned to Prabhavati and said, "My dear girl, wherever I go I see nothing but your good fortune. I hear that that letter was sent by your lovesick husband—to you." Prabhavati smiled.

"First things first. What happened with the parrot? Where is it? Why did you let it go? Why didn't you bring it to me? Don't pretend to be so smart."

"I heard from the parrot that your husband, in his intense yearning for you, wrote a letter in my name. I was so overjoyed that I let the bird go. We're lucky that the letter didn't fall into someone else's hands. That's what matters. Forget the parrot."

Sucimukhi turned to Ragavallari. "That's how the letter goes, right? Haven't you two read it?"

Ragavallari had to agree. She reported everything she had read, verbatim. "Then this silly girl grabbed the letter from my hands and wouldn't let me read any further," she complained.

"Wait a minute," said the goose. "It's not right for us to read any further. He may have written many words of love that no one else should know. It's *her* letter. A lover's thoughts are only for the beloved to enjoy. Let her read it by herself. What's more, any man who could write 'Pra-Pra-bha-bhavati' instead of 'Prabhavati' must be totally lost in love. He could write anything! And it's none of our business.

"But you know what amazes me? This man who listened as if unmoved while I was going into raptures over the beauty of this woman—a minute later writes to say that he's fallen madly in love. But then he's young, after all. Were he to remain indifferent when a beautiful woman is being described, his heart would have to be made of iron, or rock, or diamond.

"I'll tell you what I think. If Prabhavati, born with all the signs of luck on her body, doesn't achieve her wish, then the Sastra texts are no more than a deadweight for scholars, not worth believing."

Prabhavati broke in. "Exactly what wish have I achieved so far? My worry is not diminished even as much as a mustard seed placed beside a pumpkin. In fact, I have a new worry now. That supremely gentle and delicate young man is tormented on my account. The king will never accept him as his son-in-law. He won't even be able to enter this city unless the king allows it."

Sucimukhi replied, "What you said is right. Still, there is a way to get your father to allow him in. I know it. Find the right moment to tell your father about me—that I'm a masterful storyteller, highly intelligent and skilled, capable of providing a fascinating diversion to pass the time. Have him invite me to his presence. God will take care of what happens next. For now, good-bye. Don't worry, I'm not going far. I'll be somewhere in these ponds and pools. You can call me anytime you need me." Taking her leave, she went her way.

Sucimukhi Meets the King

Prabhavati went home with her girlfriend. Meanwhile, Vajranabha had dismissed his courtiers and gone into the inner palace, where he was being entertained by women singing and dancing. Prabhavati approached, smiling a daughter's loving smile, and he was happy to see her and began to speak to her with deep affection. Snuggling close to his throne, Prabhavati subtly changed the subject of their conversation. "You know, Father, there is this goose who comes to play in the pool with the others. I've never seen or heard anyone like her. She's a flying encyclopedia.

She has a name, Sucimukhi.
In eloquent speech, in inventing
new stories, in giving good advice
and in profound erudition, we've never seen
her equal. You simply must test her
yourself."

He indulged her. "Have her come here, we'll have a look." And he sent a maidservant to bring the goose.

Prabhavati, with the goose beside her, said: "Sucimukhi! My father is eager to hear you discourse on some topic. Pick something from the Sastras."

In a voice mellifluous as a gentle shower of honey, without faltering, without throwing in filler words, very gracefully, the goose made a highly learned presentation. She discussed Kanada's scientific theories, the logic of Gautama, Sankhya philosophy, the grammatical theories of Patanjali—that wise and famous serpent—Jaimini's treatise on ritual, and Vyasa's *Brahma-sutra*. She raised philosophical objections to various points, in the best tradition of debate, and then smashed them so as to establish the correctness of her theories. She proved the arguments she was making by incontrovertible deductions and lucid intellection, but in discussing her imagined opponents' theories she laid bare such flaws as inadequacy of application and various logical fallacies. She also demonstrated her proficiency in poetry, dramaturgy, poetics, music, and erotic science.

The king was ever so impressed and kept saying, "Wow." Then he asked her, "You've been everywhere. Have you seen anything of special interest that I should know about?"

The goose pretended to think hard. "I've seen many remarkable things. I'll tell you about one that impressed me most of all. I saw an actor named Bhadra who put on a performance in an assembly of certain sages, and who amazed them so much that they bestowed upon him an even greater mimetic skill. Now he travels through the universe." Sucimukhi described at some length the astonishing feats he could perform.

The king was more than curious. "I'd like to see him, too. You're quite a performer yourself, dear goose. I'd be very appreciative if you could bring that actor here." The goose promised to do so and took her leave of the king.

Prabhavati walked a few paces with her to see her off. Before leaving, the goose said to her in confidence, "My dear girl, I'm doing this for your sake. Remember me kindly."

Back to Dvaraka

With this cryptic comment, Sucimukhi took leave and flew off to Dvaraka to inform Krishna that Vajranabha had appointed her to accompany Bhadra to his city. She also told Krishna what Narada had predicted, that is, that Gada and Samba would marry the two daughters of Vajranabha's brother, Sunabha. Krishna immediately decided that these two should go with Pradyumna on his mission, as his assistants. Sucimukhi then set off for Indra's city to report on all these matters; but on the way she stopped at Pradyumna's house. She found him prostrate with the fever of lovesickness for Prabhavati and tense from waiting for the goose to bring back some word from her. She spoke with him in private.

"Did you send me a letter via a parrot?"
"Yes I did. Did you get it?"
"It reached the person you meant it for."
"Is that girl well, sweet goose?"
"You could say so—now that she's received the letter."
"What was wrong with her before she got it?"
"Why did you send the letter to begin with?"
"Because I'm in love with her, and hurting."
"She was hurting just as much, for you."
"But how did she know me enough to want me?"
"Parvati gave her your picture."
"Why did she do that?"
"To show her her husband."

The goose answered point by point, and in this way Pradyumna learned that Prabhavati loved him, and why. Then Sucimukhi said a little accusingly, "I tried to tell you back then when I described her beauty, but you didn't say a word. So I left it at that. Your silence cost you all this pain.

"Prabhavati treats me as her bosom friend, so there's no secret of hers that I don't know. I've seen, heard, and understood it all. Once she saw your picture, she couldn't take her eyes off it and stood there, transfixed. She must have been overwhelmed by feelings such as wonder and astonishment. She drank you in with her eyes, and though I can't tell you how deeply your beauty was imprinted on her mind, I can see, young man, that it keeps surfacing as goose bumps on both sides of her breasts.

"All day long she daydreams about kissing you and hugging and so on and so forth. At night, for all her shyness, you can see her playing at resisting your delicious touch—the moment she closes her eyes.

"I don't know exactly
what crime you committed
when you were making love to her

in her dream. It must have been
something awful. She was so angry
that since then she's sworn off sleep,
just to avoid meeting you. Her eyes
are open all day and all night.

"On fire with love, her body, grown thin,
glows from within. It's not for nothing
people call her a golden doll.

"She can't tolerate anything that intensifies passion.
So she won't do up her hair—
It reminds her of the bees.
She won't talk to her girlfriends.
They sound like cuckoos and parrots.
She won't look in the mirror.
She'll see the full moon.
She wears no jewels or ornaments.
They have the colors of the Love-God's arrows.
In a word, she doesn't think of anything
anymore, except for one thing.
You.

"There are moments when she gathers up her inner forces and sets off courageously to find you. Then she sees you hovering in the space before her and, flustered, turns back.

"People around her were really getting worried. She was literally wasting away. If your letter hadn't turned up at that very moment, she would have died. So the letter arrived in the nick of time and saved her life, for the time being. On the other hand, it's made things worse. You know why? Before that, she had only her own suffering to deal with. Now she knows that you're suffering, too. Every minute is as long as a year. Anyway, women can't be kept waiting too long. They're like a drop of water on a leaf stirred by the wind. You should attend to her without delay. Much depends on your intention and on her good luck."

Pradyumna said, "I want to see her now. If only I had wings to fly me to her father's palace. . . . But no one can enter there without his permission. That's what troubles me. Weren't Indra and Krishna thinking of some plan?"

"Let me worry about that part," said Sucimukhi. "Krishna already has a plan. I've worked it out that you will be sent to deal with Vajranabha, so that you can pursue your personal matter at the same time. Krishna will summon you and give you your orders. I'm going to brief Indra and then I'll go on to Vajrapuri to facilitate matters." And with this, the goose took off.

Pradyumna was preparing himself for both war and love.

War called up images of elephants, chariots,
bows and arrows, and the conch blown to declare victory.
Love presented him with his lover's breasts, her thighs,
her curving eyebrows, darting looks, smooth neck.
In his mind, they came together as similes
for one another.

THE WARRIORS ACT

Krishna summoned Pradyumna, Gada, and Samba and told them of the task awaiting them—to kill Vajranabha, who had grown insolent because of Brahma's gift, for the good of the gods. He explained how strong he was and how impenetrable was his city; and he laid out the strategy he had planned with the help of the goose: Pradyumna was to enter the city in the guise of the famous actor Bhadra. Gada would serve as his sidekick, and Samba would be the clown. Each of the three was happy to accept the mission because each assumed, unknown to the others, that it was a lucky opportunity for him, and him alone, to meet with his beloved.

Excited, they put on their costumes. Accompanied by courtesans and musicians with their *vinas*, flutes, and drums—exactly like the ones Bhadra's troupe carried—they set off. They reached the suburbs of Vajrapuri and started giving performances, showing off their skills. Word spread.

Soon Vajranabha heard about them and invited them to the court. They arrived at the theater with all their props, ready to go.

Meanwhile, Sucimukhi had already informed Prabhavati, Candravati, and Gunavati of their husbands' imminent arrival. She gave them hope to keep them from wasting away entirely under the strain of love. At the same time she kept on inflaming Pradyumna with accounts of Prabhavati's constantly growing passion for him. Secretly she moved back and forth between them, until the moment

came when she could say to Pradyumna, "Today your beloved will
be coming to see you perform." She even pointed out the window
from which she'd be watching.

Vajranabha sat in state in the royal pavilion together with his
clansmen, friends, and advisers. His wives were seated invisibly in
the screened-off women's section. He was relaxed and ready to
watch. Pradyumna took the stage as the auspicious chants were sung
for the benefit of the gods and, assuming the role of Stage Manager,
performed the opening rites.[2]

The courtesans started off singing with the heavenly *ga*-based
scale.[3] Then the cymbals and the *vina* and the flute joined in, followed
by drums pounding out their *dhim dhim dhim* in the even and synco-
pated rhythms that are so hard to follow.[4] Pradyumna recited the
nāndī blessing, before the conversation between the Stage Manager
and the heroine and the preface to the story—commonly called *pras-
tāvana*. Then they put on several well-structured plays beginning with
The Descent of the Ganges. Pradyumna masterminded a brilliant performance that included the roles of Bhagiratha and others, the natu-
ralistic downward flow of the Ganges, the realistic illusion of mountains like Kailasa, various forests, animals, birds, and so on. They created an entire world, so palpable and visible that the spectators could
not decide if it was fictive or real. Overwhelmed, the audience gave
all its jewels and ornaments to the actors. The gods who were watching from heaven were delighted to see their enemies relieved of all
their wealth.

In every role he played, Pradyumna was
that role. At other times he looked like Bhadra.
It was magical. But to his beloved as she watched,
he was always himself. As they say, there's nothing
magic cannot do.[5]

Pradyumna kept sneaking looks at the window that the goose
had pointed out, through which Prabhavati's face was visible. In his
joy at seeing her, he began speaking to her in cryptic words that
seemed to be addressed to the king. "Your Highness, you are the
most discerning of all in taste. You have chosen the very best for your
company. It was my good luck that your splendid eyes have fallen
on me. Today there's no one luckier than me.[6] The goose you sent
told me of your deep love for me. From that moment on I have been

thinking only of presenting myself before you to bring you delight. My desire is great. Take me as your servant. Tonight."

She heard and, overcome by shyness, withdrew her face, which was breaking out in goose bumps, from the window.

Standing beside her, Sucimukhi said, "So you got the message your lover was hinting at. I can see by your face."

"What hint? He said it too openly—that he loves me, and that he's coming tonight. It's all too clear. He doesn't seem to care if anyone is listening. He must be crazy. I couldn't believe my ears. Anything could happen now."

The goose reassured her. "My lady, your husband is very skilled with words. Don't worry on that account. He spoke in such a way that you thought he was speaking to you, but the king thought he was addressing *him*. The meaning you understood has no meaning for anyone else.

"When a word has more than one meaning, my friend,
the one determined by context
is the only one that comes to mind.[7]

So you don't have to worry about anyone else suspecting the meaning your husband intended for you. What everybody understood was that, in the course of offering the usual praise for the king at the end of a performance, he was taking leave before returning to his quarters." And Sucimukhi showed Prabhavati how Pradyumna was, just then, taking leave of the king, exactly as she had said.

This explanation by the goose gave Prabhavati real pleasure. Together with Ragavallari, she headed toward her palace, her mind rushing toward the impending meeting with her lover.

WAITING

She kept staring at the sun,
waiting for it to set,
and her eyes grew red
with glowing desire,
so red that they colored
the sun itself.

The sun jumped into the ocean
like a Yogi taking his ritual bath
at day's end, and the sky was
the ochre robe he hung up to dry
and the stars, the drops of water
that splashed as he dove.

Darkness spread through space.
The women of the sky
were celebrating Love's festival
with showers of black musk.

There was white in the east
and the first stars appeared.
Indra's white elephant[8]
was sprinkling a fine spray
from its trunk.

The moon rose, with its dark spot
shining in the middle,
as if the dark woman who is Night
were reflected in a polished mirror
held by her servants in the east
as she makes up her face.

When you sow seeds, you keep them in a pot tied by bamboo sticks and ropes to a flat wooden plane that is pulled across the field by a bullock; as the wood levels the field, the farmer shakes the pot so the seeds fall through its holes. Now think of the moon as a silver pot, think of its rays as the ropes, think of Love as the farmer and the minds of men and women as the fields ready for seed.

Moonlight flooded the whole world,
as if the woman called Night had filled the silver pot
that was the moon with milk that she poured
over the head of the dancing god, Siva,
who is space.

With smiles brighter than moonlight
and eyes glittering like those of the cakora birds
who feed on moonlight, young girls

selling flowers in the market
were looting young men of their hearts
and their money.

A young girl from the palace was bringing flowers to Prabhavati. A swarm of bees hovered over those flowers. One of them was the masterful magician, Pradyumna.

Prabhavati had been busy all afternoon giving orders for the perfect arrangement of the bedroom, the bed, and the pleasure palace. She was dying of anticipation. Sensitive to her moods, Ragavallari prepared her for a sensuous bath. She soaked her hair with *campaka* oil, smeared her body with perfumed powders, and then washed away the oil with fragrant myrobalan. Then she bathed her fully. She dried her with soft towels and wafted incense through her hair. Then, weaving in flowers, she played at various hairdos,[9] doing them and undoing them. As she was working, she said to Prabhavati,

"If you let your hair down, you look beautiful.
When you let it hang halfway, you look beautiful, too.
If it gets tangled, you're beautiful in a different way.
If you comb it down, even more so.
You can braid it, roll it into a bun or better still
tie it into a knot on the side.
You're beautiful with that hair any which way.

"It's long, black, and so thick
you can't hold it in one hand.
No matter how you wear it,
you'll trap your husband with your hair."

At this, Prabhavati turned around and hit her friend with the flowers she was holding, her eyes angry and smiling.

She asked for a mixture of camphor, aloe, and musk, prepared according to her wishes, and had herself covered with it together with saffron and sandal before they rubbed it all off. Then she tried different kinds of dots on her forehead—a small round circle, another one shaped like a tiny green leaf, another like the full moon, or like the new moon, or like a pumpkin seed. Then it was the turn of the ornaments— toe rings on the second toe, then the fourth toe, then the big toe,[10] anklets, belts, rings, bangles, armlets, necklaces, earrings, and so on. She tried them all on, took them off, tried them on again. There were many varieties of each of them, each more brilliant than the other, and better still when she put them on. That's why she kept changing them over and over.

She tried on a whole collection of saris—silk with golden borders, yellow with shades of red, one covered with waves with an edge like lightning in the monsoon, some with breathtaking shades of green, others with checked print. She was never satisfied for more than a few seconds. Which would her husband really like?

Finally, since nothing pleased her, she settled for a little glow of red betel on her lips, the inherent brilliance of her skin, a pair of earrings, a single strand of gold around her neck, the natural fragrance of her hair, and a delicate white sari.

But still she was restless, for she had doubts about whether she could attract her lover. She held the mirror in her hand again and again, fixing what was already perfect. Then there was the matter of the bedroom to occupy her attention. She checked out the decorations in front of the pleasure palace to be sure that the courtyard was sprinkled with sandal water. She examined the freshly covered ground and the newly painted threshold designs.[11] She ran her hands over the bed with its crafted singing birds, the saffron mattress, the golden silk pillow. She inspected the braziers smoking with aloe incense, the flowering treehouses, the screens, the pots filled with perfumes and boxes of sandal powder, the betel-nut boxes, and other accessories to pleasure.

At this time she received the flowers that the palace girl had brought. Pradyumna let himself loose from the swarm of buzzing bees and came to rest in the Nelumbo flower that Prabhavati was wearing in her ear, without anyone taking notice.

Prabhavati couldn't wait any longer for her dilatory lover. She summoned Sucimukhi and Ragavallari, who were as close to her as her own breath, to a private space and turned to Sucimukhi:

"Where is he? How can my heart bear
this heaviness? Each moment is long
as a year. Why is he delaying?
Is something stopping him?
If he were really planning to come,
he'd have told you, wouldn't he?
Maybe someone figured it all out
when he spoke to me so directly
at the end of the play.

"Or maybe at that moment he did mean to come. But after all, no outsider can get into this inner palace. But then you said that he's a man of great powers. Even the most ferocious guards couldn't keep him out. If he really wanted to, he'd have come.

"He did say he'd be here tonight.
He got me all excited, but now his mind
may have turned to another woman.
That's how men are.
They waste the feelings they arouse.
Never trust a man.

Still, he's a good man. I shouldn't blame him. I have my bad luck to blame. But how can I survive this blaze of moonlight?"

The Moon Is to Blame

She turned to the moon. "I had great hopes. I trusted you to cool me down. They call you 'Lord of Coolness,' but it's only an empty title. What do you gain by this betrayal? Just turn off the heat. It'll be as good as cooling us. They say not breaking the pots of cold water is as good as setting up a fountain.

"You sit so close to the third eye of Siva that each moment you get hotter and hotter. You were born from the ocean, still broiling in the heat of the Submarine Mare. Each new-moon day you come closer to the sun, so you're always in flames. You've taken into you the hot dying breaths of lovers traveling far from their wives. You share with your brother, the poison from the sea, the gift of scorching the whole world. In short, you've made yourself incandescent—just to fry me.[12]

"People say that you start off every month by giving the first and second parts of yourself to Fire and the Sun, to make them your friends. That must be only to take their heat so you can hurt lovelorn people like me. Hurting others is the criminal's delight.

"To tell the truth, it's a complete illusion to think that you're cool. By nature you're hot as hell. I can prove it to you. Those *cakora* birds eat your light. If it was really cold, how could they also dine on fire?[13]

"Or maybe these are bad times. Everything is upside down. Even the gentle southern breeze feels hot to me. Probably it's because it's been contaminated by your friendship."

Now it was the turn of the southern breeze. "You breathe life into everything that lives. How can you torture me like this? If the fence eats the crop, who is there to be on guard?" She tried every way she could think of to make the wind stop parching her. She tried begging and blaming. Finally, she said in frustration, "You come from the quarter of Death, so you're far from being cool. Or it's because the south is home to Rudra, the terrible god, so you're far from being cool. Fire rides you, so you're far from being cool. The snakes that live on the Malaya mountains feed off you,[14] so you're far from being cool. I'm giving up my illusions. You can't find a Brahmin home in an Untouchable colony.

"Or here's another theory. The snakes
on Mount Malaya really did eat you up,
but you didn't die. The God of Love
pumped into you the long dying sighs
of lovers left alone, and revived you.
That heat doubled yours."

━━◆◆━○━◆◆━━

Deep as the ocean,
Generous as the tree that gives all wishes,
Loyal to the king he served—
Such was my father.

━━◆◆━○━◆◆━━

This is the fourth chapter in the book called *Prabhavati-pradyumnamu*, composed by Suraya, son of Pingali Amaranarya. All great scholars celebrate his poetry and sing of his modesty.

Chapter Five

Amaranarya was always conscious of consciousness itself,
the fruit of worshipping Siva with
fruits and flowers.

THE LOVERS MEET

Prabhavati turned her attention to the Love God:

"Mind-born god, son of Rukmini,
you're no other than my lover,
Still you haven't given up the habit
of having no body.
It's my bad luck.
I don't want to say anything against you.
I hesitate even to mention your name.
I can only pray to you."

Even as she spoke, her pain and longing were becoming unbearable.

"That day he sent me a letter that saved my life. Today he took the trouble of coming to this city and appeared before me. He said in public that he was coming to meet me, but in the end he let go of all that."

Her eyes were rolling upward and her throat was parched. "Son of Rukmini, I want you for my husband even in my next life." She moistened her lips as she spoke these words. She was about to fall onto the bed of flowers in her death-agony. Now Love emerged, in his true body, from out of the Nelumbo flower behind her ear.

"Don't give up now. I'm here, my dear. I'm your husband. Look at me." He lifted her from the bed and embraced her. At the enlivening delight of his touch, she quickly revived, but then fainted again in extreme happiness. Then she came back, her eyes wide open, staring at her husband with shyness and a certain hesitation. She released herself from the hands that had longed, so long, for this moment, and ran into the inner room.

A little bewildered, Pradyumna looked at Sucimukhi and Ragavallari. "This woman is the fruit of all the good deeds I ever did, in all my lives. Is it right for her to run away after winning me over? I can't bear this delay. Go bring her to me. The two of you will be witnesses to our private wedding."

Ragavallari laughed at him. "You heard how devastated she was by your absence. You can't blame her now. She's simply too shy to appear before you. She's drowning. You're the expert on love. You know what to do."

Sucimukhi added, "You know all there is to know about women of every sort. Still, let me tell you, as best as I can, about this girl. She was openly wanting you. When she realized that you knew that, she became shy. Now she's run away because she wants you to catch her and bring her back by your own power. This is what's called 'hiding with the back in view.' It's her deepest desire. If you think she's made a mistake, just remember it's only one of her ways of showing love. Don't think she doesn't want you. The two of us will go and bring her back."

Ragavallari and Sucimukhi went behind the curtain where Prabhavati was listening to this conversation. "Some woman you are," said the goose. "Do people run away from their lovers? If your husband's mind turns cool, what will you do then? Think it over."

Ragavallari turned to the goose. "She's only shy because we're here. She'll be fine if we go away. She's no fool." Then, to Prabhavati, "When your lover is full of passion, you shouldn't delay. Feelings don't stay at the same pitch all the time." She grabbed her by the hand and started pulling, but Prabhavati wriggled away. Ragavallari burst out laughing. "No matter how much you resist, you can't hide your secret. Everyone knows. You sang your love from the rooftops. It's too late now. What's more,

"Your husband is listening over there. How stupid can
    you be?
Is this the best way to be shy? If he thinks you don't care
    for him,

you'll be helpless. He's a perfect lover, and he knows
   everything.
He'll follow your mind. There's nothing to fear.
   And remember,
we have to hide this. Delay could be risky."

She coaxed her, comforted her, threatened her, and, in general, gave her a lesson in the etiquette of such occasions. Having softened her up, she took her by the hand and pulled hard.

Still, she resisted. She was dragging her feet, too shy to go forward. "Wait a second," she said, "there's something I have to tell you." But she had nothing to say; she just swallowed the words. Every step was a battle. Ragavallari was pulling, and Prabhavati was pulling in the other direction, holding tight to every doorknob. She totally exhausted Ragavallari with these delaying tactics, though she was, at the same time, very worried that her friend would give up on her and go away. That's how young girls are on their first night with their husband.

Lucikly, Ragavallari knew her friend inside out, and she knew what was best for her. Still, it was like dragging an elephant to the post. A major effort.

But she got her there at last. Of course, Prabhavati had another attack of overpowering shyness and tried to hide behind her girlfriend. She was trying her best to overcome it, but in vain. Because she was bursting out in goose bumps and sweat, her makeup—the beautiful crocodile designs all over her body—was melting and running. She was struggling to get away from her place in front of him, and in the struggle her blouse slipped again and again from her shoulders, exposing the fullness of her breasts on both sides. She was reluctant to look at him directly, so her eyes, which were long enough to reach her ears, kept flitting restlessly to the side as she turned her face away, to the great good fortune of her usually all-too-neglected cheeks.

Ragavallari pointed at the girl in this hapless state and said to Pradyumna, "This is how young girls behave. Until now she's been asking for your love openly. She made every effort to get you here. Now that you're here, she's playing hide and seek." As she spoke, she brought their two hands together.

The prince took her and married her on the spot in a *gāndharva* wedding, which requires no further ceremony. Still, the goose chanted a few mantras: *ayaṃ muhūrtas sumuhūrto 'stu*, "May this moment be auspicious," and so on.

For a split second, husband and wife stood still, taking in each other's touch and forgetting the rest of the world. Meanwhile, the inborn feminine qualities of timidity and shame were coming out. "Swear you won't leave me!" she cried to her two friends.

That was the moment they chose to leave, each making some excuse.

Pradyumna brought his cheek close to hers and whispered in her ear, "My dark-haired beauty, your friends are leaving now. Why do you want them to stay? Am I not your friend, too?"

Prabhavati paid no heed.
She was trying to get away.
He held her in a big circle formed
by his hands. "Off you go," he said.
She turned around, looking for a break
in the circle. Her thighs, arms, breasts,
braid, ears, and cheeks brushed against him
again and again.

"You're exhausting me," he complained,
"by this pretense of shyness." Now he took firm hold
of her hands and made her stand still. He flicked the drops
of sweat from her cheeks with his fingernails. Then he stroked
her body.

Wanting to steal a kiss on her cheek, he whispered empty sounds into her ear. He lifted her face toward him and combed through her curls with his fingers. He pretended to find interest in specks of dust on her sari; what he really wanted was to touch her breasts. Aiming at the knot that tied her sari, he rubbed the jewels on her belt. He shooed away what was left of her shyness and embraced her, at last, with extreme gentleness, awaking her. The knot untied itself.

With his hand pressing against her cheek, he kissed her. He carried her to the bed. By this point her resistance had become rather feeble, and he knew it. First he drove her a bit crazy with various external procedures, and then little by little by little he made love to her, as much as she could stand.

They lay on the bed, content,
entangled in one another
like two garlands of golden campak and black
water lilies intertwined.

DAWN

The morning star appeared in the east
like a diamond that tops a red flag
unfolded for the sun.

The Yadu prince woke and at once
tightened the embrace that had gone slack
in sleep. Pressing his cheek against hers,
he woke her. She opened her eyes, saw him,
closed them again.

Then she half opened them. To keep her husband from seeing her naked, since her sari had come loose from their love, she brought her cheek against his face—this produced a certain thrill—and while embracing him with one hand, she freed the other and, feeling for one end of the sari, brought it over her breasts, held it there, and went searching for the other end under her buttocks, following their curves. When she found it, she lifted her waist slightly and pulled the cloth under and through, joining both ends at the belly button. Holding her disheveled hair in place by lifting her shoulders, she tried to get off the bed. But she was too beautiful for Pradyumna to resist, and he drew her back and held her tightly to his chest.

There were things he had to do. He put his lips on her ear and whispered, "From now on I'll come here every night. But I have to spend the daytime hours in my lodgings. Otherwise, our secret could come out, and our plan will be blocked. I'm making a tunnel from here to my place, and that's how I'll leave. Close the entrance to it when I'm gone so that others won't see it." Prabhavati excitedly nodded approval.

Pradyumna left through the tunnel, and Prabhavati closed its trapdoor. The cock crowed, as if uttering a mantra and specifiying, as is usual, its meter, its time of application, the sage who received it, the deity who presides over it, and its use: "*vividhaṃ chandas triyāmântar antimayāmo bhagavān ṛṣiḥ kusumadhanvī devatā māninī-ramaṇāyāṃ viniyogaḥ,* that is, Composed in various meters, to be uttered in the final watch of the night, with God Himself as the sage and the God of Love as the deity, this mantra is used for making love to proud women." It produced immediate results. All over the city, proud women begged their husbands to make love.

Dawn appeared in the east, like new growth from a tree that had been cut down the day before, like a red tent pitched by the vanguard of the sun's army proceeding against the forces of darkness, like metallic dust kicked up by the demons who always fight against sunrise, like a red screen held up for the entrance of the goddess Sri as she begins her daily dance on the lotus flowers.

Brahmins lit bright fires for the morning oblation, before sunrise, and the flames reflected off the full breasts of their wives, sitting near, far brighter than the early-morning sunlight reflected from the reddish wings of the *cakravaka* birds, mating at dawn. The sun rose like a fiery red ball that the Lady of the East took in her hands as an ordeal to prove her faithfulness to Indra: "Not even in my dreams is there another man for me. You are my only lover. If you have any doubt, just look."

Prabhavati, meanwhile, was looking at herself in the standing mirrors. At her breasts that still showed the marks of her husband's armlets. At the scratches left by his nails on her body, still glowing with the dried-out flakes of sandalpaste. At her cheeks bearing the impress of his earrings, and her lips that showed his bites.

Sucimukhi and Ragavallari reappeared, smiling. "Someone hasn't quite woken up, it seems. There's still time. Don't rush to spit out the betel you've been chewing all night. We're in luck—we get a glimpse of your sleepless body, sleepy eyes, dried sandal flakes." They came closer. "You haven't brushed your teeth or put on fresh turmeric or washed your face. You haven't changed your clothes or done up your hair or put the dot on your forehead. You didn't put on fresh mascara or your jewels. None of your morning prayers has been uttered. This is the first time this has happened. You must be very tired from last night. Or maybe you're enjoying the signs of love on your body. Did we come at the wrong moment?"

Embarrassed, pretending to be angry, Prabhavati pushed them away with her fingers, and this excited them even more. At this juncture, Candravati and Gunavati arrived as if to say hello to Prabhavati, but really hoping to find Sucimukhi and to invite her to their houses to help them concoct a plan for meeting their husbands.

Prabhavati was flustered to see them arrive without notice, since she hadn't had time to put herself together.

They saw her. Some small doubt budded
in their minds. They examined her carefully,
inspected all the evidence, and came to the firm conclusion

that she'd been with a man. They smiled,
exchanged knowing looks, and with light in their eyes,
unable to hold the thought in their minds, they spoke
to one another so she could hear.

"There's a certain new beauty
in her body. Have you seen it?
Her eyes tell us she hasn't slept.
Something special must have happened.
One should be happy when something
comes to fruition."

They poked and teased her with words. "Whatever happened has happened. You've done it. Just tell us how you managed to be so lucky in this heavily guarded palace?"

Prabhavati turned pale. For fear of revealing the secret, she had no idea what to say. Sucimukhi took stock of the situation. She quickly decided that there was no way out of the impasse except to tell Prabhavati about the other two girls and their boyfriends. In the long run, this would be the best course for them as well. The goose weighed all the pros and cons of it in her mind and, choosing her words carefully, said to the two visitors, "Why are you making such a fuss? Prabhavati read the same book you read. She just got the results a little sooner. After all, she's slightly older than you."

Prabhavati sent an eager glance at the goose. "So you have them on your hook as well! Tell me how it is. Clearly."

The goose laughed. She could see the two girls frantically signaling to her with their eyes, to keep her quiet. Prabhavati, on the other hand, was invoking the gods, demanding that Sucimukhi talk. So the goose said to the girls, "It's your own fault. You don't know how to keep quiet, do you? Haven't you heard that when you comb hair looking for lice eggs you might find a full-grown louse? Now she's invoked the gods and I have to tell her your secret." And Sucimukhi proceeded to reveal the whole story beginning with the parrot who had carried the letter from Pradyumna and including the entire affair of the two girls and their Yadu lovers.

Prabhavati smiled at her friends, who were holding their heads low in embarrassment. "You liars! You were covering up the whole affair and chasing after me? Don't say another word. We're in the same boat."

"Dear friend," said the goose, "you may be in the same boat, but they're not quite your equals. If you don't intercede with your husband on their behalf, they'll never meet their lovers. But if you're too shy to speak about this with your husband so soon, I'll tell him, today or tomorrow, with your permission."

She got Prabhavati to signal agreement with her eyes. Looking at the two daughters of Sunabha, Sucimukhi said, "The fine man who married Prabhavati has superhuman gifts. Your husbands won't be able to get into this palace except through his good offices. That's why I thought up this plan.

"Stop worrying. You can tie your husbands to the end of your saris. I'll make them come to you tonight." And the goose had Prabhavati send the girls back home, their heads bent in shyness but with a smile on their lips.

Two More Secret Weddings

The goose went that night to where the actors were staying and took Pradyumna, Gada, and Samba aside. "We can't get anywhere until you've taken care of your personal matters," she said. "I'll have nothing to report back to Indra about our mission." This set each of them thinking. "This goose seems to suggest that in addition to the mission Indra gave us, each of us has his own personal agenda." Each was wondering what the others' secret could be.

Sucimukhi knew exactly what was going on in their minds. "Each of you is probably quite unaware of the affairs of the other two. Just listen." And she revealed all three love stories to all three of them. Then she looked at Pradyumna and said, "You're a tricky one. You found a way to your girl. Your two friends, however, are in agony. They can't find a way to their heart's desire. It's all in your hands now. You think of a plan."

They were smiling at one another and teasing each other now that the secrets were out. "And I thought you were totally focused on Indra's mission! You had me fooled. You came here for the girl."

"Right, and what about you?"

Pradyumna looked at the goose. "Go tell the girls that their lovers are on their way." He told Gada and Samba about his secret tunnel and sent them off. As for him, he went back to Prabhavati.

Every time he tried to kiss her,
she would turn her face away.
When he would aim for her cheeks,
she would cover them with her hands.
He would pull the cover off her breasts,
and she would cross her arms to hide them.
If he pulled off the cloth below,
she would tightly cross her thighs.
Her reserve drove him to want her more
and more. They made love
for some nights.

"I'll get over my reticence. Tonight. I'll satisfy my desire.
I'll embrace him first, pressing him to my breasts,
hold him, bite his lips." That was her daytime fantasy,
but all night long her tyrannical shyness
held her back.

The Yadava hero taught her gradually, very carefully, all the ways of making love. Then he crowned her Queen of Love's Remarkable Kingdom.

In the beginning she would falter while making love on top, no matter how much her husband begged her. By the end, she was so impassioned that Desire possessed her.

The heaviness of breasts and buttocks, far from being impediments, enhanced her joy as she moved. The former, round as *cakra-vaka* birds, pulled upward. The latter, round as wheels, pulled her down.

He wants to stare at her breasts, but the wish to
*   embrace her takes over.*
He wants to embrace her, but the idea of caressing
*   her buttocks takes over.*
He wants to caress her buttocks, but he also wants
*   to straighten the hair on her forehead.*
More than he wants to straighten her hair, he just has
*   to kiss her lips.*
More than everything, he wants to make love to her.

Even more than making love, he really wants to kiss her.
That's the thing about making love. One move
    precludes another.

Prabhavati pleased him. As for Candravati and Gunavati, they were secretly married, by the authority vested in love, to Gada and Samba. Nights passed in increasing abandon.

Some days were spent on stealing an embrace,
    a kiss, a caress.
Some days went on intensifying pleasure by gently playing
    at resistance.
Some days free access was permitted, as if by accident.
Some days a curtain of shyness only increased their curiosity.
Some days there was no holding back, and the jingling of
    their ornaments
mixed with full-throated love moans, as if bells were ringing.

A SLIP OF THE TONGUE

And one day

as Prabhavati was making love to him with all the skill at her command, Pradyumna was so overcome that he cried out, "Rati,[1] my life— I'm totally yours!" He said it with true love, and the name hit her like a spear driven into her ears. If at a time when a couple is engaged in the very depths of loving, after long days of yearning, the man lets slip the name of some other woman, it's a little hard on his partner.

The incomparable excitement that had suffused Prabhavati's whole body just a minute before turned into anguish. For women, the name of a rival, uttered at such a moment, is like a death knell.

She froze. Her pride shattered, she sighed heavily and turned away, facing the other side of the bed. Then she got up and went to another bed. Pradyumna tried to approach her, saying, "My sweet, what's going on? Did I do something wrong?" She invoked all the gods, ordering him to stay away.

Now it was his turn to sigh. He stood still, tortured by being separated from such a beautiful creature. He began to talk in tones clearly audible to her where she lay, her face turned the other way. "Was there some mistake on my part? Or are you just testing my patience? Or do you think it will be more fun to make love after a little spat? Is there some real reason for you to be angry, to get up and leave?"

Still suffering deeply, she gave no reply but only sighed again.

Pradyumna, his mind very agitated, went on. "How have I offended you? You're really in pain. You are my life. Would I ever do anything to hurt you? Please let me come near so I can convince you. Kindly command me to approach you. Or, if you prefer, come to me and ask me any questions you want. If I really did something wrong, is there any way for me to wriggle out of it? You can tie me up with your waistband or put my neck in a vise. I'll gladly go along."

Prabhavati made a great effort to keep her voice from shaking and to get the words out straight. Pradyumna, for his part, hung on every syllable. "Sir, who am I to ask you questions? You did nothing wrong. What's wrong in thinking about people whom you can't remove from your heart? Come to think of it, it's my fault that I'm still alive after what I heard. I got up from the bed because I'm still sadly attached to my body. Your false words of love seem to put me at fault—and I should probably blame you for that, though I don't want to. Actually, I should accuse you of only one thing—of making me swim through space with your seductive words. You are capable of cutting throats with a soft wet cloth. These empty, glib sentences are always on the tip of your tongue. You seem to think that I'm Rati, your beloved queen. Lord, I'm not that woman Rati. For your information, people call me Prabhavati."

She was inflaming herself with her words, sobbing and weeping and crying in deep, low tones: "What kind of life is this for me?"

Pradyumna understood at last. It was all because he had cried out Rati's name at the height of passion. He smiled. "My dear, I didn't realize until this moment. Is that why you're so angry? I was simply saying your *rati*, your skill in lovemaking, is super. Any problem with that?"

All she heard was "Rati is super." That's how it is when something sticks in your mind. There's no room for anything else. She kept rolling the phrase around inside her: "Rati super Rati super Rati super. . . . Why did he have to rub it in?" she was thinking. "I know he loves her better than me. She is truly super, but why say it in words? It's clear from his actions."

Pradyumna had another go. "Talk to me. Let me hear your sweet words—at least one syllable. You don't seem to hear me, or to care how bad I feel. You invoked all the gods to prevent me from coming to you. You're far away from any kindness, even though you're close enough to know that I'm in pain. It's true you're perfect in all other ways but this: there's no kindness in your heart. After all, you're the daughter of a demon.

"And since you yourself, my lovely girl, are so very angry at me, it's hardly surprising that the gentle breeze and the moon are also torturing me with their heat. The Love God is hurting me, and *he* happens to be *me*—and anyway, a person who causes suffering to his lover only hurts himself.

"Let go of your oath. Let me come close and soothe you. Or you come here and let me drink at your lips."

As he was begging her, he heard music on the street, in the distance, from outside his lodgings. "It must be time for Vajranabha's soldiers to wake up the king," he thought. "If I don't leave now, my mission will be ruined." He got up and made for the tunnel he had dug. She ran after him, forgetting her anger, feeling the pain of imminent separation, like someone who wanted to scare but was scared herself.

He did not notice that she was following him. He left hastily via the tunnel for his residence, his mind intent on other things. Prabhavati came to a halt at the entrance to the tunnel. Afraid to advance further, her mind aflame, she turned round and went back to the bed where her husband had been lying. She found his sandals there—the sandals that had the good luck to touch his feet—and pressed them to her breasts. She smeared all over her body the flakes of sandalpaste that had fallen from his chest. She touched the discarded garlands of flowers to her eyes. For a while she was happy.

She remembered his astonishing beauty that she had experienced firsthand. She thought about the way he made love. She imagined the depth of his love. She conjured up his tenderness.

"How could I get angry at such a man?
Especially when he was talking about my skill
in making love, as he subsequently
explained. At that moment I misunderstood
and refused to listen. I was deceived
by my fate.

If I think about what he said in his letter,
am I not lucky to be so loved?

It's all my fault. He was begging me,
and I wouldn't listen.

Men are like bees, they say.
They go from flower to flower.
But in his case, considering the intensity
of feeling and the boldness of his words,
to say nothing of the letter,
there's no room to find fault."

BACK TO THE LETTER

By this time, while she was rolling around in torment, day had dawned. Prabhavati retrieved the letter that she had hidden from all other eyes, the letter she worshipped as if it were the god of her house; taking it with her outside to a private corner of the lovers' garden, she began to read it to herself in a low voice, starting from the place Ragavallari had left off. Even though she had read each line many times before, still it was as fresh as the first time.

"Dear goose. My life is in your hands.
Bind my heart to hers and make them one.
Kindly take this letter as if it were ten thousand letters.
Tell this woman in my very words:
'My lady, alive like the lightning in the sky,
if you hear me, I'll be proud of being me.
My name is Pradyumna. To rule all three worlds
is worth less than the tiniest fragment of your affection.
I'll obey the merest glance of your eyes.
I'll take any vow you demand.
If I hear that you're indifferent to me,
that same moment the Love-God's flowers will kill me.
So while I'm still alive, let me tell you how I hope
to kiss your honeyed lips, and how I hope
to bathe in the moonlight of your smile, and how I hope
to put my cheek on yours, and how I hope
to caress your buttocks, and how I hope
to crush your breasts against my chest, and how I hope
to touch you everywhere, and how I hope
to hear your moans, and how I hope

to press your thighs.
These fragrant flowers in my garden,
their fresh honey, these gentle breezes,
the open moonlit spaces—they will absorb me
after melting me down to the five elements.
You know, don't you, that they're the enemies
of a suffering lover? The full moon
is a friend of your face.
The cuckoo's call is a slave to your speech.
Streaks of lightning remind me of your movements.
Black bees are the servants of your dark hair,
as bright buds serve your lips,
as the lotus takes lessons from your eyes.
All these give me joy—but only if you take my hand.
They are death to me if you turn away.'
Dear goose, tell her what I'm thinking,
and write me back whatever she says.
I'll be waiting to hear."

As she was reading, her lover listened, too,
having crept up behind her,
taking these words to heart.[2]

Prabhavati, however, was reliving the meaning of the letter, word by word. "Until a minute ago, no one was as fortunate as I. But tonight I ruined everything with my baseless anger. I distanced myself from him. Now no one is more unlucky than I."

Ragavallari appeared. She caught sight of Pradyumna standing motionless behind Prabhavati but, reading a signal from his eyes, she pretended not to have noticed him. "You're looking rather pale today," she said to her friend. "You seem to have forgotten your morning routines. You're as thin as the moon at the end of the dark fortnight. I see stains of mascara on your breasts. The cooing of the cuckoo startles you, and a cool breeze makes you faint. And just where did you get that letter you're hiding between your breasts, under your sari? Is it the one your husband sent you that day? Why be so shy about it? Does it mean something different today? That's what your face tells me. Husbands are never faithful to their wives."

As she spoke, Ragavallari kept glancing at Pradyumna. Guided by his eyes, she went on: "Your husband must have exhausted you tonight. It's quite clear. You can't hide it. You have so much love for him; you shouldn't be angry. Anyway, you had no real chance to be angry. You're like someone who pretends to be losing in order to make her partner go on playing. Look how you're suffering ever since *he* got angry. Actually, he was only pretending to be angry. He just wanted to see how beautiful you look when you're on fire. But don't worry: your ever-so-skillful lover won't be able to stay away for long."

Ragavallari appeared to be speaking to Prabhavati, but in fact she looked straight through her and said, "You son of a cowherd! What a fine lover you are! Should we declare you unfaithful to our friend? You've found a new honey, and you want to have a taste. Am I right?"

Prabhavati protested. "Watch your words. Don't say a word against my husband, that supremely compassionate man. Didn't I tell you that I caused the whole problem with my insane anger?" And she proceeded to tell Ragavallari the whole story of how she was upset and turned away from him, up to the point when Pradyumna left. She was going on and on, reproaching herself, and becoming exhausted in the process from the pain of separation. She lay down on a cool slab of moonstone and pulled Ragavallari toward her head, so she could use her lap for a pillow. Ragavallari, taking advantage of the moment, signaled to Pradyumna to take her place while she slipped away, smiling.

In her anguish, Prabhavati didn't notice. Resting her head on the lap, she started to say, thinking Ragavallari was still there, "My dear friend, I'm dying. This is the last time we will meet. Remember me in good times." She sent a hand up in the direction of the neck and pulled the face down toward her. Suddenly she saw it was her husband's face next to hers. Bashfulness, surprise, and happiness flooded her. For a split second she froze, like a painting.

Pradyumna said, "Why are you so surprised? I'm your husband, am I not? I went away because I had some business to take care of—and anyway I wasn't able to console you—but then I realized that the matter was not meant for today, so I came back as fast as I could. I've been standing behind you, watching everything."

He took her arms and lifted her up so she was sitting up on his lap. He combed his fingers through her curls, pressed his cheek against hers, kissed her lips. Holding her closely from behind, he touched her breasts. "Promise me you'll never get angry at me again," he said, biting her lips and pressing his fingernails against her breasts. "*You* promise *me* that you'll never make me angry at you again," she said, biting him back and pushing hard against him with her firm breasts. Anger had momentarily built a dam against the rising tide of their desire, but now the flood broke through it—a thousand times stronger than before. There are no words to describe the way they made love now; it was all the more passionate because of that hurt pride.

THE SECRET REVEALED

Pradyumna and Prabhavati enjoyed one another for a long while. From time to time Pradyumna would perform for Vajranabha, captivating him with his skill. As for Gada and Samba, they made love to Candravati and Gunavati, respectively, every night. During the shows, they helped Pradyumna out by playing the clown and the sidekick, among other roles. The king of the demons liked them, too.

All three young women missed their periods. Their bodies grew weak, and they had a flat taste in their mouths. In the mornings they felt ill. Their cheeks grew pale, and their nipples became dark. Their waistline thickened. The three folds of flesh below the navel disappeared. They were, in short, very pregnant.

Nine months later, on an auspicious day, Prabhavati gave birth to a son. They called him Prabhavan. Candravati gave birth to a boy whom they named Candraprabhu, and Gunavati had twins, Gunavan and Kirtiman. The newborns instantly became young men, well educated in the Vedas and the Vedangas, and also superb archers. They lived with their mothers in the palace. One day, Vajranabha heard of their existence through their guards. Enraged, he assembled his court.

"Can you see how our times have turned crooked?" he cried indignantly. "Those rascals who sought their pleasure in my house are using the fangs of the thousand-headed snake, Sesa, to scratch their back; or you could say they're trying to fry peanuts in the fire of Siva's third eye.

If they are sons of the gods, today is Doomsday
for heaven. If they are snakes, the world of snakes
will end today. If they are human, this is earth's
final hour.

We have to catch them alive and destroy them along with the world they came from. You go get them," he ordered Bhimabala, the city's Chief of Police.

Bhimabala went and did not come back. The king sent, one by one, his best generals and, finally, the Commander in Chief. When they all failed to return, he figured things out. Their heads were hanging from the ramparts of his fort.

Vajranabha went to war. Aflame with rage, together with his brother Sunabha and his ministers and friends, with chariots, cavalry, elephants, and infantry, he surrounded the women's quarters. The earth shook under their feet. Pradyumna, Gada, and Samba were in the actors' quarters. They knew that if they delayed, the young boys in their mothers' palace would not be able to face the fearsome demon; so they quickly went through the tunnel and rejoined the women, who were gathered together in one place, very frightened. They reassured them and praised their young sons, who appeared with swords soaked with the blood of the demon soldiers they had already killed. Pradyumna looked at Prabhavati and said, "My dear, your father is invading us. There is danger at the door if we don't enter the war. Battle is no ball game. Nobody can tell what will happen when we start fighting. We can't choose whom to kill. My sweet, I can't see if there is sadness in your face. Your father won't stop his violent ways unless he's killed. If I enter the battle, there's no other way to go. What shall I do? I'm troubled at heart."

She looked intently at her husband, who was torn at the prospect of having to kill the demon king. From where she stood she could see her father already scaling the walls with his heavily armed soldiers. She tried to find some other way to save her husband, her children, and herself. Finding none, she cut her love for her father from her heart.

She went herself and brought the sword from the corner. Placing it in her husband's hands, she said, "Kill the king of the demons. Doubt no more. No more."

Pradyumna, pleased at her words, stationed Gada, Samba, and the four sons to guard the women while he himself ran out of the palace, flourishing his sword, to lift the siege of the fort. With its high golden walls, the fort looked like Mount Meru; Pradyumna circled it, blazing like the sun. The demon's soldiers ran away as darkness flees from light. Pradyumna attacked those who were trying to scale the walls on rope ladders. Vajranabha, impressed by his boldness, faced him and said: "Who are you? No one can enter my city without my permission. Brahma gave me this boon. So how did you get in? I'll settle accounts later with Brahma and his false promises. Right now, I'm coming to teach you a lesson. You and your family will perish."

Pradyumna was unfazed. "You'll be able to settle accounts with Brahma only if I let you survive. You are ruined by your own evil. Brahma never lies. You yourself let me into your city when I came as Bhadra, the actor. I am Vishnu's son, from the Yadava clan. My name is Pradyumna. I married your daughter by my choice. The men who married your nieces are my people. These young, invincible boys were born to them and to me. They're guarding the women in the palace, and they're the ones who killed your commanders.

"If you take refuge with Vishnu and Indra, I will not kill you. If you don't, my sword knows no kindness, as you will learn all too soon."

"You can say what you like—because I and only I allow you to stand before me." Vajranabha showered him with arrows.

Gada and Samba saw it all from inside. Furious, they opened the doors of the fort and rushed out at Sunabha and his army. Meanwhile, Vishnu heard about the fight from his geese-messengers. He came with his brilliant discus and other weapons, illuminating the sky, and Indra happily joined him. Indra offered his chariot, well equipped with bows and other weapons, driven by his charioteer Matali, to Pradyumna. He also issued armored chariots to Gada and Samba. Though energized by these gifts, the Yadava heroes were still not quite a match for the demon army. The fight dragged on with blows and counterblows until Krishna, watching Vajranabha's skill, concluded that victory might still be a long way away. He sent his discus to Pradyumna's hand, and Pradyumna used it to cut off the demon's head.

Elated at Pradyumna's triumph, Gada and Samba broke Sunabha and the other demons into pieces. Flowers fell from the sky. The gods beat their drums, and there was the usual dancing and singing.

Now that it was all over, Krishna spoke kindly to the citizens of Vajranabha's city, who were rather distraught at the loss of their king. He divided the country into four parts, one for each of the four boys. After crowning them, one by one, Krishna sent Indra back to heaven and took his family—his sons, Pradyumna and Samba, his brother Gada, and his daughters-in-law and sister-in-law—back to

Dvaraka. There Pradyumna played endlessly with Prabhavati while remaining ever devoted to his father, who is God.

This story comes from the Hari-vamsa.
It tells of the goodness of Krishna's son.
May God, Lakshmi's lord, give fame to my poem.

⊳⊷⊶⊙⊷⊶⊲

Pingali Amaranarya was my father. He nurtured those who served him and supported all who are good. He spoke the truth gently and profoundly. This book is for him.

⊳⊷⊶⊙⊷⊶⊲

This is the fifth and final chapter in the book called *Prabhavati-pradyumnamu*, composed by Suraya, son of Pingali Amaranarya. All great scholars celebrate his poetry and sing of his modesty.

Afterword
The Sixteenth-Century
Breakthrough

INDIVIDUALITY

We have argued for the evolution of a radically new sensibility in late sixteenth-century Andhra, one informed by a growing sense of the individual and the singularity of experience. You can clearly hear the new tone already in the very first, invocatory verse of Suranna's book.

Uma and Siva
became two halves of a single body
because they wished to show each other
how thin they'd grown
from missing one another
when they lived apart.
Their love is ever new.
May that loving couple bring fame
to the lord of this book.

The poet is praying to Siva and his wife, Parvati, who together form an androgynous unity, the Ardha-narisvara, and asking this combined form of the god to bless the memory of Suranna's father, to whom he has dedicated the work. The iconic form involved is a familiar one. What is new is the motivation the poet offers for its coming into being in the first place. The androgyne has an emotional logic. In

Suranna's imagination, in contrast to what the iconographic texts tell us, there is no original androgyny in this god. Rather, there are two separate individuals who love one another and who have become emaciated because of being separated. Moreover, they seem to need to communicate this sense to one another. Hence their fusing themselves into a single body without, perhaps, entirely losing their separate identities. They are now together because of an act of personal choice. Finally, their love for one another is not a uniform, unchanging state of mind but rather constantly, playfully renews itself—*ati-vicitra-vilāsulu*. *Vicitra* suggests invention and surprise, perhaps the dominant feature of this relationship.

This is far from the standardized themes of desire in classical Indian literature. Raw desire or sexual pleasure (*rati*) is regularly idealized and abstracted as *śṛṅgāra*, a refined eroticism. Hundreds of classical and medieval texts in Sanskrit and the regional languages work through this theme with immense variation. The poeticians tell us that *śṛṅgāra* is produced by the appropriate configuration of conditioning factors, *vibhāva*, secondary expressions, *anubhāva*, and concomitant, transient emotional states, *vyabhicāribhāva*. In the theoretical synthesis of Abhinavagupta, following on Anandavardhana and others, *śṛṅgāra* is a *rasa*, a generalized and depersonalized "flavor" to be experienced by the listener or audience of a poetic text or play. Thus poetics becomes a form of audience psychology applying especially to those moments when the listener has so divested himself of any residual individuality that the latent, undifferentiated universal *rasa* (in this case, *śṛṅgāra*) can rise to the surface of awareness. The key notion here is *sādhāraṇī-karaṇa*, "universalization," literally, a "making common" that overwhelms personal consciousness and produces the wished-for, collective aesthetic effect.

On a certain, rather superficial level, Suranna follows all the conventions authorized by tradition to produce this effect. He exploits the erotic potential of his theme within the confines of *kāvya*-style descriptions of the hero and the heroine, including the inevitable stages of their love and lovesickness, the recycling of traditional metaphors—sometimes rather strikingly extended—and of standard topoi (such as the lovers' reproach to the full moon, the cool breeze, and the god of desire). Telugu scholarship has been rightly appreciative of Suranna's achievement in evoking *rasa* through carefully crafted verses, in line with all that an educated, refined reader would naturally expect.[1] Everything is thus in order; Prabhavati and

Pradyumna, in Suranna's hands, admirably embody the classical types, remorsely going through their predestined paces.

In fact, external appearances to the contrary notwithstanding, they do not. *Śṛṅgāra* in the sense just discussed is an erotic relationship between an idealized man and an idealized woman—who could be any young and beautiful man or woman. But Suranna's Prabhavati and Pradyumna are self-driven, subjective individuals, each developing in his or her own way, and as such—only as such—do they fall in love. Perhaps we need a new term to explain the novel aesthetics of texts like this one—*pratyekī-karaṇa*, "intense individualization," would convey what we mean. The intensification of the individual presence is what makes the texture artistic. To perceive the change that has occurred in the terms and conditions of a love story, one needs to pay close attention to nuance and evolving characterization.

Take an example. Sucimukhi, the eloquent goose, is ready to begin her verbal portrait of Prabhavati for the benefit of Pradyumna, who is hearing of this girl for the first time. Here is how the goose introduces her exquisite subject:

nĕttammul' añcu krŏnnĕlal' añcu vaṭa-phala-śrīl añcu,
    tābeṭi cippal' añcun'
ammula pŏdul' añcun' anaṭikambamul' añcu pulinam'
    añcunu suḍi cĕluvam' añcu
hari-madhyamamb' añcu haima-kumbhamul' añcu
    nava-mṛṇalamul' añcu civurul' añcu
madanu śaṅkham' aṭ' añcu maṇi-darpaṇamul'
    añcu pagaḍam' añcunu tila-prasavam' añcu

śapharul' añcu singiṇul' añcu candra-khaṇḍam'
añcu śrīkāramul' aṭ' añcun' aḷul' aṭ' añcun'
iṭṭivi gadayya cĕppa boyinan upamalu
vini taḍava sigg' ŏdavun' avvĕladin ĕñci (2.63)

What images can I marshal
to describe the beauty of her body, from toe to tip?

Lotus blossoms, crescent moon, banyan fruits,
tortoise shell, a quiver of arrows, banana plants,
sandbanks, whirlpools, a lion's waist, golden pots,
fresh lotus stalks, leaf buds, the conch of the Love God,

jeweled mirrors, red coral, a sesame flower,
darting fish, a bow of horn, a piece of the moon,
the curves of the letter Sri, black bees—

It's a shame we can't do better.

Pradyumna is offered a list of all the standard similes for parts of the
female anatomy: her feet are like the lotus, her toenails like the crescent moon, her ankles like banyan fruits, and so on. Prabhavati,
imagined through these clichés, would be exactly like every other
beautiful woman in Indian poetry. Of course, the goose complains
that these similes (*upamalu*) are insufficient—so much so that she
feels embarrassed to have marshaled them. The poetic means
she has at hand are, she implies, utterly impoverished. Nonetheless,
because these are her only available verbal resource, she describes
Prabhavati, part by part, in more or less the same terms—although
several times in the succeeding verses she again protests the inadequacy of the comparisons. Such statements denying the efficiency of
the familiar simile are nothing new. There is a name for this move in
Sanskrit poetics: the trope known as *vyatireka*, "excelling," in which
the subject of comparison outdoes the object or standard of comparison, sometimes to the point of ridicule (*pratīpâlankāra*). It is also not
at all uncommon for a *vyatireka* to be extended to the point of denying that language can portray the subject altogether.[2]

But Suranna has actually gone a step beyond these familiar
usages. The bizarre juxtaposition of such well-worn similes in a run-
on series has the effect of rendering the entire enterprise, not just the
trope itself, ridiculous. Reading or hearing the verse, one tends to
laugh. A rich irony takes hold. Moreover, the poet's lexical choices—
including such rather crude, utterly unpoetic words as *tābeṭi cippalu*,
"tortoise shell"—effectively caricature the inherited tropes. Their
very standardization, which tends to depersonalize and abstract,
now seems out of place. In a way, this verse is an indictment of the
state of the art. See how little a poet can do when a particular, individual beauty has to be described.

The problem is not that Sucimukhi lacks facility with words. She
was trained by the Goddess of Speech herself and was even crowned
with a fine title: *upamâtiśayokti-kāmadhenu*, "Mother of Similes and
Hyperbole." The goddess herself had this title engraved on an anklet
that she tied with her own hands to the goose's foot, as Telugu kings

were said to do for their favorite court-poets.[3] Nonetheless, as the goose clearly states, all of this mastery fails at the critical moment.

I can try my best to describe her, but I can't touch
even a billionth of her beauty. Don't conclude from this
that I'm any less of a poet. I'm the best when it comes
to language. Speech herself trained me to be as eloquent
as she. (2.89)

We could restate the poet's problem, which is shared by Sucimukhi and Pradyumna: How can anyone describe a specific individual, marked by idiosyncracies of character and appearance, by means of the available linguistic stock? A poet—or a lover—has to cut through conventional language to visualize the beloved. In fact, this is what Suranna makes Pradyumna do in the immediate sequel to this passage. The goose has gone off, leaving Pradyumna sick with love and desperately trying to conjure up the image of Prabhavati in his mind:

He was unable to divert his mind from the unique and stunning vision of Prabhavati that could be clearly seen in the mirror of the goose's words.

With rising desire, following the words of the goose,
he intensified the beauty of the images she had used,
like "bees" or "moon," a thousand times over.
　　He composed the girl
in his mind out of hair, face, and all the limbs of her body
as far as he could imagine. Finally, he got a glimpse of her
in his inner eye.

In this way he went on without pause
connecting each of the images to the proper part
of her perfect body and magnifying the beauty of the similes
a thousand times over, to the limit thought
could reach. He saw her exactly
as she was. There is nothing beyond the grasp
of an unfettered mind. (2.107–109)

Pradyumna is endowed with the "pure" or "unfettered" mind (*acca-pu buddhi*), free from any external encumbrance or contamination, that allows him to visualize something or someone in exact, realistic form. We should take a moment to consider the term. In the internal economy of consciousness in medieval South Indian texts, *buddhi* is generally far from pure. Experience, desire, misperception, ego-investment, karmic residues—all these obscure and limit the operation of *buddhi*. True perception is normally broken up by unavoidable obstacles. Yet, in theory, a lucid, unfettered mind could see through the opaque and distorted surface of reality. It is, in fact, possible to see things as they are—given a certain ability to focus and, more important in the present context, to free the imagination from its chains.

Here we touch a central theme in Suranna's innovative meta-psychology. An active imagination, pushing at reality, shaping and thus truly seeing it, enables Pradyumna to complete his task. Of course, he still needs the given images and linguistic devices, which he intensifies many times over, seeking the singularity that he knows must be Prabhavati's. A major element is the process of connecting or composing the various parts of the beloved: Pradyumna is working with, or working on, the linguistic materials the goose has provided; he "connects each of the images to the proper part of her perfect body" (*tat-tad-avayavatva-susthitiki tārpaga*, 110), composing the girl in his mind (*madik' andina yantayunun nayiñci*, 109). The result is that he sees her with his inner eye "exactly as she was" (*ammadirâkṣi-rūpam' ĕyyadiy adiye kānambaḍiyĕn*, 110). So the entire sequence is one of visualization fueled by desire and dependent on the recomposition or reintegration of discrete linguistic figures and their bodily correlates, powerfully heightened by the imagination to the point that they become almost transparent. In the end, Pradyumna sees *through* the goose's metaphors to a living reality that these same metaphors have, at least initially, rendered accessible to imaginative perception. We will return to this point.

If we have any doubt about the sequence or, in particular, its verbal and figurative components, Sucimukhi herself can put it to rest. In the course of her description, she raises, only to refute, the possibility that she could paint Prabhavati's picture instead of resorting to words:

> You might suggest that I try to paint her likeness and show it to you. But to paint any one part of her body, you first have to contemplate it; and the moment you think about it, your mind is lost in her beauty; but then there's no way to paint with a distracted mind.

What's more, if it were possible for a person to replicate her in painting, this implies that the Creator God—for example—could have created some other woman like her, somewhere else. But Brahma himself once admitted, in my presence, that he didn't create her. It was the First Goddess, Parvati, who made her with her miraculous artistic skill.

Prabhavati, that is, is unique, resistant to any available artistic reproduction, yet somehow present to Pradyumna's imagination, apparently his most important faculty.

On the other hand, Prabhavati, for her part, fell in love with Pradyumna *after seeing his portrait* as painted by the goddess Parvati. So visual art does have a role here, one complementary to or symmetrical with the imaginative act of visualization. Let us attempt to make sense of this contrast, which reaches to the heart of Suranna's understanding of artistic production.

Obviously, it is not a matter of sheer beauty. In Indian poetry, beautiful lovers are usually beyond description. They also may conform, more or less, to the standard paradigm of lotuses and tortoise shells. In Suranna's case, as already hinted, the central concern seems to be with the notion of recalcitrant particularity. Prabhavati is, no doubt, beautiful, but she is above all beautiful in her own way. This is the real problem with referential language or other means of representation. It is this singularity that regularly eludes articulation. Pradyumna's painted portrait, however, has very little, if anything, to do with representation. The goddess has painted it herself and given it in a dream to Prabhavati. The portrait is entirely real: it walks right out of the dream and occupies space in Prabhavati's garden. Prabhavati is even too shy to look at it because of its overwhelming, realistic presence. The next stage, we might say, is for Pradyumna himself to walk out of this picture in all *his* individual concreteness, with the marks or scars that are uniquely his (the impressions of Rati's bracelets, the scars on his chest left by Sambara, and so on), all eventually described by our poet.[4]

Bhāvanā

Such a move happens more than once in Suranna's poem. What should be "only" a picture, or a dream, or an actor's role, becomes a full-fledged, living person. Artistic form first replaces or supersedes the unimagined surface, then intensifies itself to the point of generating a tangible presence. There is always an interactive element in this process. The viewer or listener is integral to the effect. Thus, Prabhavati studies Pradyumna's portrait with a certain intensity that entails a necessary progression:

> When the picture arrived, she looked at it and saw the young man in all his captivating gestures and movements, as if emerging from her own determination to behold him, out of the depths of her own feelings. She stared at it head-on, then from an angle, her eyes wide open, then half closed, her shifting moods overwhelming her as she watched.
> "I thought I'd be satisfied just by seeing it, but the longer I look, the more excited I become. It's something new every moment. He won't let me take my eyes away. I can't stand it."
> Overcome, she rushed at the painting and embraced it.

She will soon discover that the painting is not her lover's actual presence, yet this is hardly the point. Prabhavati seems to be seeing right through the painting—to the real person. To a large extent, this vision is the result of her own determination (*ātma-saṅkalpa-vāsanā-viśeṣa*), her intense visualization that reflects some inner decision. We need to listen carefully to the subtle semantic shift evident in this compound. In prior usage, *vāsanā*, the final element in this psychic economy, is an unconscious karmic memory or "fragrance," activated at critical moments to produce the experience of déjà vu. We all carry untold *vāsanās* of this sort within us, awaiting their activation through some unconscious triggering. But here *vāsanā* follows upon *saṅkalpa*, "determination," a clear statement of intention: Prabhavati first *intends*, then experiences the effects of that intention, the "fragrance" of her own feelings. This single pregnant phrase shows us an inner world that is crystallizing anew.

What is more, the lover she sees in her mind is changing every moment. He is hardly a stable, iconic entity; and it is this very dynamism and continuous movement that captivates her and will not let her go. The quality of attention required is also remarkably dynamic, shifting its perspectives: she tries looking at the painting directly, then from an angle, then with eyes half closed, and so on. Each new vantage point gives rise to a different mood (*bhāva*), and these moods intermingle and overwhelm. Notice the sense of a complex but somehow unified awareness active under conditions of emotional "overload" and, in particular, under the organizing control of the subject's own will and purposefulness.

Prabhavati's clear intention—*ātma-saṅkalpa*—has its precise analogue in Pradyumna's mental system, the "pure mind" (*accapu buddhi*, discussed earlier) that allows him to reconstruct his beloved in all her uniqueness. In both cases we are dealing with the mind's power to make something real, to bring something into existence—what we have translated by the Western term "imagination." For example, the lovelorn Pradyumna, still replaying the goose's description, manages to "create Prabhavati's full presence in his imagination" (*bhāvanā-balamuna manamuna ghaṭitam agu maguva madhurâkṛti*, 3.16). *Bhāvanā*, the imaginative faculty, is not, in this case, suggestive of illusion, of creating something unreal (as in the modern romantic usage). On the contrary, *bhāvanā* is a true perception of what is real and a materialization of that reality in one's own presence—in fact, a realization. *Bhāvanā* manifests, shapes, motivates, and names. It is not a generation ex nihilo but a visionary intensification of a piece of reality to the point where it achieves distinct contours and some measure of autonomy. Desire plays a part in the process, as does intention or determination.[5] This kind of "imagination" has to be integrated into the new profile of the person that Suranna is expressing. Intensely individualized characters depend on it for their very existence; imagination is what allows them to reach out to one another. Without the potential for *bhāvanā*, for the creative shaping of reality in line with a visionary perception, the sixteenth-century individual could not act or interact. If we want to use a word such as "subjectivity," we have to begin with *bhāvanā*. The world is real yet not merely given; it comes into being[6] in the course of being perceived. But even within these terms, within the truly creative field of a lucid, imaginatively active mind, there is still room, or need, for linguistically mediated communication: our two lovers cannot actually meet without the help of the goose Sucimukhi, "Perfect Speech."

Suranna, as we have noted, inherited this Sucimukhi from his *Hari-vamsa* source, but he has clearly developed her role far beyond anything in the earlier text and also deepened the meaning of the name. Perfect speech goes with the unfettered mind capable of realizing a singular presence. If imagination individualizes—and this seems to be its primary force—speech connects: Prabhavati and Pradyumna seem, in fact, to communicate best, without misunderstandings, through the goose. Sucimukhi allows

them to see one another as they are. In a sense, Sucimukhi speaks
for the poet himself and serves as his self-portrait: she, too, has
been trained by Sarasvati, the goddess of speech, and she thus
fully commands the tropes and other expressive means of language, as we know from her courtly title, "Mother of Similes and
Hyperbole." Apparently, if speech is to produce reality, it has to be
intensified through such devices.[7] We have already mentioned
Suranna's keen interest in precisely these creative effects operating
within language; his two other works, each in its own way, are
devoted to this theme. What stands out in *Prabhavati* is the definitive embodiment of the creative voice or word in an individual
character, a second, internal narrator, who constantly comments
on and reports to the various figures within the story and to both
the poet and the reader outside it.

There is another metapoetic presence central to our story, that
of the actor, Bhadra, whom Pradyumna impersonates in order to
enter the sealed city. The original Bhadra had won a boon from
Brahma—the actor's dream that "when he acts, no one will be able to
tell him apart from his role" (2.27).[8] Pradyumna, disguised as this
Bhadra in his performance for Vajranabha, retains this gift and, at the
same time, goes well beyond it.

In every role he played, Pradyumna was
that role. At other times he looked like Bhadra.
It was magical. But to his beloved as she watched,
he was always himself. As they say, there's nothing
magic cannot do. (4.102)

There seem to be three layers to Pradyumna's appearance: he is
Pradyumna himself—only and always himself—in the eyes of
Prabhavati; then he is guised as the actor Bhadra; and, as Bhadra, he
entirely merges with each of his roles. Prabhavati alone may be
assumed to see all three—to see through the roles and guises that
cast a spell over the rest of the audience. More important, however,
is the fact that she always identifies him as himself. Perhaps a more
general statement is implied, as the quoted line at the close of the
verse would indicate.[9] There is nothing magic cannot do, just as there
is nothing beyond the grasp of the unfettered mind. As earlier in the
text, when Prabhavati's decisive intention allows her to see through
the painted portrait to the real existence of her lover, here, too, she

penetrates external guises by virtue of her love. An empathic or imaginative identification emerges out of the artistic shell or form and generates true perception.

In another sense, however, Prabhavati may well be blind to the illusion of the theater. When Pradyumna makes his exit with a speech in double entendre—at once flattering Vajranabha and setting up a tryst with his beloved—Prabhavati hears only the deeper level, the one relating to her. She completely misses the surface level and has to be instructed by Sucimukhi about the determining force of context for language. Once again, "perfect speech" is needed to interpret the lovers to one another. Public language, the language of surfaces, is heavy with illusion. A "true" imagination that sees through any given surface, is not.

There is a palpable consistency to these themes as they appear in Suranna's book. A concrete, tangible painting is given in a dream— and survives the dream. (In the introduction to the book, Suranna mentions a great-great-grandmother of his who was given a *dŏṇḍa* vine by the Sun-god in a dream; her family, in waking life, exfoliated like this vine with generations of offspring—1.15–16.) Pradyumna learns of Prabhavati through Sucimukhi's description of her and, enhancing the images, sees her actual presence. Prabhavati sees through the painting to the irreducible individual with whom she is falling in love. She also sees through her lover's masks when he is performing as the actor Bhadra and hears his double-edged message as intended only, and literally, for her. To these instances we may add one more, somewhat unusual in its layering effect and the uneven movement through perceptual layers: the impatient, lovesick Prabhavati begins a tirade against the Love-God, Manmatha, as is usual in all such *kāvya* texts; but she stops short, in the middle of the verse, when she realizes that Manmatha and Pradyumna are, in fact, the same person (her husband-to-be).

"Mind-born god, son of Rukmini,
you're no other than my lover.
Still you haven't given up the habit
of having no body.
It's my bad luck.
I don't want to say anything against you.
I hesitate even to mention your name.
I can only pray to you." (5.3)

Once again, a surface level present in all artistic forms—dreams, paintings, theater, and also everyday language—opens up to reveal a concrete personal reality. Stated differently, a process of conflation or superimposition that begins with the conventionalized image of the god expands to include his identity with Pradyumna and ends by focusing on Pradyumna, not the mythic alloform of the love-god but the palpable human identity, alone. Unfortunately, this utterly human figure is temporarily absent, thus confirming in Prabhavati's eyes his mythic attribute of being bodiless. Manmatha, that is, is also Pradyumna—no, he is, for present purposes, *only* Pradyumna—but this human Pradyumna, being physically absent, is thus bodiless Manmatha again.

A cycle, typical of Suranna's vision, thus completes itself. One begins with some inherited or conventional name or pattern—rather like the inadequate metaphors with which the goose first describes Prabhavati to Pradyumna. This hollow name is not denied but rather fleshed out by identification with a real human being. Manmatha *is* Pradyumna. At this point Prabhavati abandons her complaint and turns to prayer; the tone is at once playful and alive with feeling. The god-lover she is praying to, or playing with, can now recoincide with his earlier mythic or conventional identity—though in a slightly ironic way. The human Pradyumna's absence *in the body* is all that matters to the woman who loves him; it is in this sense that she picks up his mythic attribute (he is *atanu*, "bodiless") and, once again, grounds it in her own tangible frustration. Perhaps this ironic literalization of a conventional perception, via a process of extreme personalization that includes a built-in distancing from the simple, given name or form, is what allows Pradyumna to materialize at just this moment:

> Her eyes were rolling upwards and her throat was parched. "Son of Rukmini, I want you for my husband even in my next life." She moistened her lips as she spoke these words. She was about to fall onto the bed of flowers in her death-agony. Now Love emerged, in his true body, from out of the Nelumbo flower behind her ear.

The bodiless god has a "true body" (*nija-rūpamu*, 5.7) after all. The question is only how to "imagine" it—in the sense of bringing it outwards (*věluvaḍi*) into perceptible form (*bhāvanā*).

We have used the language of "opening up" not by chance. The whole story centers on a demonic, illusion-ridden city that is hermetically closed. The two lovers breach its confines through *bhāvanā*, the intense perception of each other's reality as offered to them through artistic means. For this to happen—if, that is, one is going to see *through* the enchanted or crafted media—an irreducible specificity may be required. Singularity marks the deeper level and enables the transition. Concrete details, the individual quirk or gesture, make all the difference. In this respect, the aesthetic emerging in Suranna's late sixteenth-century Telugu text stands in the sharpest possible contrast to the classical poetic theory of *rasa* and *dhvani*, with its preference for an idealized and prototypical "universalization."

The autonomy of perspective follows this same logic. What one sees when one truly observes is an irreducible, context-dependent, entirely unique perception. Beauty flows from the cumulation of such perspectives. To generalize or abstract from a particular context is to destroy the uniqueness of what is perceived. Take the following remarkable description of Prabhavati's prototypically long, black hair (as described by her friend, Ragavallari, who is doing up Prabhavati's hair in preparation for the first meeting with her lover):

"If you let your hair down, you look beautiful.
When you let it hang halfway, you look beautiful, too.
If it gets tangled, you're beautiful in a different way.
If you comb it down, even more so.
You can braid it, roll it into a bun or better still
tie it into a knot on the side.
You're beautiful with that hair any which way.

"It's long, black, and so thick
you can't hold it in one hand.
No matter how you wear it,
you'll trap your husband with your hair." (4.131–32)

A verse like this—realistic, perspectivist, wry, witty, and highly personal—is unprecedented in earlier South Indian literature.

Privacy

Behind the classical *kāvya* template, with its set features and natural progression, its patterned language of longing and eventual fulfillment, stands the emergent individual of the late sixteenth century. If we take Suranna's portraits as a basis for generalization and listen attentively to the nuances of his language, we can discern the following somewhat tentative profile. The new individual stands largely alone, notionally (though not pragmatically) freed from his or her moorings in a community (Pradyumna and Prabhavati cross "caste" boundaries when they fall in love). He or she is endowed with a particularity that matters more than any formal criteria of character or beauty and that is celebrated as such. A certain psychic coherence or integrity comes through consistently, carrying the character across changing moods and moments of doubt or crisis. "Imagination," *bhāvanā*, the true perception of reality as rooted in a visionary interiority, has literally opened up the world and serves to guarantee the distinctiveness, indeed uniqueness, of the perceiving mind. A powerful awareness of the human body and a celebration of its sensual potential animate these portraits.[10] The individual is a psychic entity whose mental life is capable of being communicated in complex language (often paronomastic, operating on two or more superimposed channels at once), reflecting the complex nature of the mind. What is more, there is a cultural interest or investment in communicating these mental contents.

The story Suranna has chosen shows us this more autarchic individual deliberately divesting himself or herself of social determination. The conventional nexus of family and clan allowed only erotic relationships that were approved by the elders. Marriages were made by the family and for the family. Passionate choices were usually depicted as charged with the seeds of potential destruction for the collectivity, even for the social order as a whole. Such instances of individual passion violated convention and set up oppositions—pitting the mother, for example, against the new wife. (A good son was expected to prefer his mother.) Traditional *śṛṅgāra* themes also usually leave the collective, clan- or family-based order intact. Men and women fell in love, in this literary universe, more or less within the confines of normative society. Love in these contexts, elaborately described and emotionally fulfilling, did not lead to dissonance. An aesthetic concept—*aucitya*, propriety—guaranteed a certain orderliness in all such affairs. Even when desire breaks the bounds for a moment, as in the case of Peddana's *apsaras*-heroine who falls in love with a married Brahmin, Pravara, the poet avoids a conflictual solution.[11]

By Suranna's time, this picture is changing, as we see from the lexical shifts in the domain of erotic love. Earlier, passionate love tended to be classed as *moha* or *kāma*—desire-driven infatuation, with some negative connotation. Love for one's mother or other members of the close family was *prema*, an affectionate condition. These two worlds were kept safely apart, linguistically as well as socially. *Prema* never impinged on erotics, nor was *kāma* used for family relationships. This division was first shattered in *bhakti* devotional contexts, which allowed *prema* to signify the devotee's passionate, erotic engagement with the god. Suranna, however, takes this usage a step further. His story is one of *prema*—erotic love on the part of one individual for another who is, as it happens, also outside the entire network of clan loyalties. Both Pradyumna and Prabhavati are prepared to risk their entire social world for each other. They can imagine a private space of their own.

Only in such a private space can the new *prema* flourish. This *prema* is an intimate emotion that can be shared, if at all, only with a trusted friend. Ragavallari tells us so explicitly at an early point in her conversation with the goose:

> "There are secrets you can't share with your mother, your sisters, or any other close relative. Such are the feelings that come when you're overwhelmed by love, which can be shared only by the closest of friends. Even if you give your life for such a friend, your debt remains unpaid." (3.88)

We should note that Ragavallari, who fulfills precisely this function of intimate friend for Prabhavati, also consistently reflects and articulates the newly evolving sensibility we have been exploring. She is, we could say, another metapoetic, feminine voice framing—in some ways also deepening—the development of the heroine; she repeatedly finds ways to make explicit the autonomous, singular, and private components of Prabhavati's experience, as in the case of Pradyumna's letter, which she literally saves from destruction at Prabhavati's hands. Ragavallari, that is, is the late sixteenth-century Telugu woman in her reflexive, self-aware aspect. As such, she advances the course of her friend's romantic love by creating and maintaining a secure, private space within which it can fulfill itself (also by insisting, in the face of Prabhavati's shyness at the crucial moment, that it *must* fulfill itself).

We want to stress that the emerging individual of the sixteenth century is not simply self-constituted by a single, autonomous imagination but is rather socially recognized and legitimated in terms of a changing collective order. He or she is a new product of social interaction. Put differently, the new domain of personal imagination is socially sanctioned, collectively patterned, and culturally shared. Take, for example, the fact that Suranna records the first private, written love letter in Telugu literature. Pradyumna sends this letter, via a parrot, to Sucimukhi, his only direct link to Prabhavati. The letter informs Sucimukhi what exactly she is to say to Prabhavati in Pradyumna's name. The instructions for delivery are very specific; there is an addressee, whom the parrot-postman has to find:[12]

> "Yes, I'm going to Vajrapuri," the parrot said. "What can I do for you? Tell me in one or two words."
> "Great bird, a certain royal goose called Sucimukhi is in that city. Find out where she lives and deliver this letter to her. That's my request."
> "I'll do you this favor," said the parrot, "but I must fly. There's no time to talk. Just tie the letter under my wings, where no one can see it. Hurry."

In fact, the postman's mission fails—the parrot is caught in a snare set by Ragavallari—and the letter falls directly into Ragavallari's hands. Notice carefully what comes next. Ragavallari reads the first part of the letter—the outer envelope, we might say, addressed to Sucimukhi:

> She opened it and began to read in a clear voice: "Greetings to Sucimukhi, who bears the honorable title 'Mother of Similes and Hyperbole' graciously bestowed by the goddess Sarasvati and inscribed on an anklet on her foot. This is a secret letter written by Pradyumna, driven by love. You spoke to me about Pra-Pra-bhavati . . ."
> Ragavallari jumped up and down in excitement, waving her arms. "Listen," she cried, "this is a letter sent by your lover to you! What luck!"
> "Is that really what the letter says, or are you just teasing me? Show me the letter." She stretched out her hand. Ragavallari ran a few paces, trying to escape her, clutching the letter. "I

swear by God, that's how it is. Let me read it through for you. You can see it afterwards."

"You're lying to me. It can't be me. Who knows who that Pra-Pra-bhavati is? Look carefully at the letter. You don't have to give it to me."

"As if you didn't know it's your name. He was so excited that he wrote the first syllable twice."

"Well—if you say so . . . Anyway, read the rest. Stop running around. I'll keep quiet."

"In that case—listen." She went on reading from where she had stopped. "'You spoke to me about Pra-Pra-bhavati. If I didn't say anything at the time, it's because I was pretending to be proud. But you described her so graphically that each of her features has been imprinted on my mind and has acquired a life of its own, as if carved in my heart. I can hardly bear such beauty. I'm exhausted by the weight of it. Dear goose, beg her to revive me with a kiss.'"

At this point, Prabhavati snatched the letter from her hands.

Ragavallari let it go without further struggle. "It's not right for me to read further, anyway," she said. "He may have written out his love in very intimate words. Save it for when you're alone."

The letter is explicitly said to be "secret" (*rahasya-lekha*), but "secret" now means something closer to "private." The term *rahasya* has also undergone an important semantic shift compared to earlier usages: for example, in philosophical or religious contexts where it usually points to an esoteric truth reserved for the initiate. Here *rahasya* is what belongs to Prabhavati's own private space. Indeed, a strong and innovative notion of privacy is in evidence throughout this passage. Prabhavati somewhat coyly suggests that she may not be the right recipient, since her name is not Pra-Pra-bhavati. Perhaps the letter was meant for someone else; accuracy is crucial when it comes to delivering mail. Ragavallari protests that the letter writer was overwrought, distraught with love, and hence misspelled the name (were his hands shaking as he wrote? Pradyumna is like any young man writing his first love letter to a girl before he knows if she will reciprocate his feelings). But even when this problem has been resolved, Ragavallari still breaks off her reading the moment the letter becomes too personal. She respects Prabhavati's privacy and advises her to read the letter herself, when she is alone. A few minutes later, when Prabhavati tries to tear up the letter, Ragavallari protests again: it is, after all, addressed to Sucimukhi, and Prabhavati has no right to tear up somebody else's letter.

Prabhavati does, it seems, read this letter privately—many, many times. She keeps it in some hidden place and retrieves it at moments of doubt: for example, after her first quarrel with her lover. She reads it to herself (*tanalo*), in a secluded place, in a very low voice (*alpa-svarambuna*, 5.151). This is not yet totally silent reading, but we are not far from it. A new protocol for reading is taking root. Until this point, reading always meant reading aloud in public, as a performance. Now it is becoming something that belongs in a private space.

The letter has two parts: the first, addressing Sucimukhi, is given to us in *sīsa* meter; the second, initially continuing this address, includes a long message meant for Prabhavati directly and is in rhyming couplets, *dvirada-gati-ragaḍa*. Both meters are remarkably close to prose (the second part, intended for Prabhavati alone, is somewhat heightened in intensity). This prosaic quality suits the personal and private nature of the communication. Note, too, that as readers we are allowed access to the second, more intimate section of the letter only near the end of Suranna's long text—as if this document, which first appears at the structural or spatial center of the work, in the third chapter, somehow brackets and contains the rest of the narrative. In a way, Pradyumna's love letter *is* the story.[13] The novel—an extended, ramified love letter moving through the public, external casing to a deeply private space—can conclude only when this final and critical section of the letter is "read out" to us by the author in all its proleptic urgency, its frantic articulation of Pradyumna's obsessive imaginings and longings. It is as if this core fragment of the text, hidden within the main story and split into two segments, has, by sheer imaginative intensity, exfoliated the "outer" events we have been reading all along.

Moreover, what is true for the love letter may well be true for this book as a whole. It is probably the first Telugu text intended to be read for oneself, not performed publicly. Unlike nearly all earlier Telugu *kāvyas*, the *Prabhavati-pradyumnamu* has no internal listener, no addressee or patron lurking in the outer frame. Earlier poets dedicated their books to their patrons, or to their god, who are formally addressed at the start and close of each chapter.[14] Thus, the *Kala-*

purnodayamu was offered by Suranna to Nandyala Krishnamaraju, his patron, described directly in flattering terms at each chapter break. We, as listeners, effectively overhear a recitation for the benefit of the patron. This format—the split frame—is, in fact, a diagnostic feature of Telugu *kāvya* generally, from its beginnings in the eleventh century.[15] In the case of the *Prabhavati-pradyumnamu*, however, this frame disappears. The poet has dedicated his book to the memory of his father, whose name appears—but never in the vocative—at the beginning and end of each chapter. The father is not actually listening to the poem. Suranna symbolically respects the inherited frame but actually does not use it. The book is really addressed to us, his readers, who are meant to read it for ourselves.

FATHER AND SON

Suranna tells us at the outset that he was motivated to compose this work to celebrate his family. In none of his previous works did he have an opportunity to describe his genealogy or, in particular, his father (1.6). Clearly, his father's memory played a role in this creative enterprise. The son is, in a way, positioning himself as his father's son and in this sense stating, or finding, what could be called an "identity." He is, first, his father's son. In a sense, this novel keeps the father alive in the author's memory; the story is told in the father's silent presence. Here the father is not a controlling figure, heavy with authority, but rather offers the son a specific locus or space within which he can express his vision. The entire genealogy with which the text opens enhances this space by providing a sense of personal origins and a specific family history. Note, also, that Suranna proudly declares that he, quite alone, made the decision to compose this book. Nobody, neither king nor god, asked him to do it (in the manner of early patrons); it was a decision of his own inner self (*ātmalona*) that took place after he had already begun the process of composition (*prabhāvatī-prādyumnam' anu prabandhamu ācariñcucun*, 1.5).

We find ourselves in the classical matrix of what we are calling the novel. Suranna has created an arena in which new subjectivities, or identities, can come into play. The courtly setting that was hitherto normative has given way to a family context, reiterated at every narrative break. It is also there right at the beginning, in the second invocatory verse, ostensibly offered to Vishnu and Lakshmi as parents of the god of love:

Couples love each other
because of Love.
That same Love was born
to the Ancient Couple,
Vishnu and Lakshmi.
None can equal their togetherness.
May they bless my father, Amaresa Mantri,
son of Pingali Surana,
with every joy.

Manmatha, Love embodied, is positioned in relation to his father and
mother, whose unequalled togetherness has created him: their love is
the same force that drives couples together everywhere. This is a
book about love. But it is also about Love in a particular, human
form. The verse reminds us of Prabhavati's attack on the absent love-
god, whom she suddenly remembers is none other than her lover,
Pradyumna (5.3): what begins on the level of a mythic name, hence
an abstraction, rapidly devolves onto a living person who coincides
with that name. This is the perceptual cycle, fueled by imagination,
that underlies Suranna's story as a whole.

At the same time, we have to remember that Prady-
umna–Manmatha as the hero of the narrative has, at best, a rather neb-
ulous relation with his "mythic" father, Krishna. Once Pradyumna has
himself fallen in love, he is markedly independent, just like Prabhavati,
who gradually cuts herself off from her father. In her case, however,
this issue of full autonomy is worked through in a remarkable process
of self-discovery that builds up to a clear moment of decision.

Remarkably, the text itself thematizes the issue of the father's
role. The narrative culminates when Prabhavati is faced with an ago-
nizing choice. Her father is at the door, eager to kill her husband, his
natural enemy. Pradyumna sensitively makes *his* dilemma clear to
his wife: if he goes into the battle, he is all too likely to kill her father.
What should he do?

> She looked intently at her husband, who was torn at the
> prospect of having to kill the demon king. From where she stood
> she could see her father already scaling the walls with his heavi-
> ly armed soldiers. She tried to find some other way to save her
> husband, her children, and herself. Finding none, she cut her love
> for her father from her heart.

> She went herself and brought the sword from the corner.
> Placing it in her husband's hands, she said, "Kill the king of the
> demons. Doubt no more. No more." (5.197–98)

Suranna presents this moment with great economy, but its existential
force comes through clearly. Earlier he has hinted that Prabhavati is
not quite the daughter of Vajranabha—she was created by Parvati.
Still, she has grown up in Vajranabha's palace and clearly sees him
as her father. Now she has to take a stand that will determine her
life's course. Prabhavati, who has lived and acted as an individual at
earlier points in the story—who has chosen her husband in contra-
vention of all social logic and inherited prejudice—chooses to save
her nuclear family. It happens very quickly, and her short statement
is one of the most moving in this book.[16]

What is it that allows this heroine to make the choice, finally
becoming the self-determining person who has been evolving
throughout the story? Apparently, love—*prema* and not the earlier
notions of refined desire, *śṛṅgāra*—motivates Prabhavati's individua-
tion throughout, as it also informs all of Pradyumna's choices. Such
prema is not simply the coming together of two individuals; it implies
the clairvoyant effort of the imagination that we have seen to play so
crucial a part throughout this story. A certain imaginative transcen-
dence of form infuses form with an aliveness that enables true connection. Given such an aliveness, derived from *bhāvanā*, both the heroine and the hero become fully present to themselves and to others in
the context of their love for each other. The sixteenth-century individual is no lonely monad. Love creates these subjective persons with
their active and eloquent interior spaces, their interwoven wholeness,
and their readiness to take risks. Conversely, *prema*—unlike the classical poeticians' understanding of *rasa*—is possible only between two
such relatively autonomous, self-aware individuals.

This is not to say that Prabhavati and Pradyumna go through a
single, parallel sequence. Pradyumna's course may be somewhat more
direct. Once he has recomposed his lover's image in his mind on the
basis of the goose's remarks, he moves unswervingly toward her. The
letter he sends, his actor's disguise, his paronomastic speech, the form
he takes in the Nelumbo flower—all these are necessary steps in her
direction. He also tells us—more precisely, he tells Vajranabha just
before engaging him in battle—that he has been following his own
instincts and wishes all along: "I am Vishnu's son, from the Yadava

clan. My name is Pradyumna. I married your daughter by my choice"
(*mad-iccha kai kŏṇṭi nī kŏmārita pŏndun*, 5.205). This strong statement of
identity, beginning with the name of his father and ending with an
unabashed assertion of free volition, is surely the high point of
Pradyumna's inner trajectory.

Prabhavati, however, seems to mature in a somewhat different
rhythm. Her great, initial gift is in seeing the living reality implicit in
Parvati's portrait of Pradyumna; she is, from this early stage on, prepared to sacrifice everything in order to find and win him. But it is only
in the final, critical moment of choice that we see her entirely self-pos-
sessed, self-aware, and capable of existential action. Following the logic
we have been pursuing, we could say that, for Prabhavati, the story
ends at the point where she can connect the formal, verbal token—the
word "husband," for example—with the fully imagined and internal-
ized individual who can now lay claim to this name.

CONTINUITIES

Suranna appeared at a critical juncture in the history of South
Indian literature, as we have already said. Although the tradition
sometimes connects him with the great period of Krishna-deva-raya
(1509–29) and its poetic masterpieces, it is almost certain that he in fact
belongs to the second half of the sixteenth century or the early seventeenth. At least one popular story about him recognizes this genera-
tional gap. Suranna is said to have been a vagabond in his youth, with
no interest in education. Because of his father's high status, a marriage
was arranged for him with the granddaughter of the great poet
Peddana (the author of the *Manu-caritramu* and a member of Krishna-
deva-raya's court). The bride, however, was well educated, and the
bridegroom became ashamed—so ashamed that he went off to Kasi to
study. When he returned, he began to compose the *Raghava-pandaviyamu*, a highly learned, linguistic tour de force. Peddana, the grandfather, asked him to recite a verse from this new text, and the young
poet proudly began to sing (*talapan cŏppaḍiy ŏppĕn appuḍu . . .* , " At that
time, if you think about it [the River in the Sky . . .]"[17]). Peddana
protested that in the very first words of this verse the poet had already
introduced four lexical breaks, at which point Suranna went on to
recite the rest of the poem—mostly a single long, hair-raising compound (*tad-udyaj-jaitra-yātrā-samutkalikā-riṅkhad-asaṅkhya-saṅkhya-jaya-
vat-kaṅkhāṇā-riṅkhā-virśṛṅkhala-sanghāta-dhārā-parāga-paṭalâkrāntambu*

[*minneru*]) that won Peddana's approval.[18] The verse as a whole offers the following picture:

At that time, if you think about it,
the River in the Sky was a thick salve
compounded of the dust stirred up by hooves
of innumerable warhorses on their way to battle,
a salve applied to the cracks that had opened up in the sky
when the royal drums shattered space itself.[19]

This story implicitly recognizes the fact of a break, not merely in lexical matters but also in the way poetry is composed. Unlike earlier poets, Suranna writes verse that reads more like prose. In this lies one facet of his originality. The tradition, however, expects a poem to flow without breaks in a single liquid movement (*dhārā*); the story thus attempts to assimilate Suranna to the poetic praxis from which he in fact deviated.[20] It is also of interest that the central image of the verse has to do with plastering over cracks. The long compound in the verse, extending across two and a half lines, is, in fact, close to Peddana's preferred style. Nonetheless, Suranna is clearly taking this style in a new direction, in this case making one text tell two different narratives (he recommends to his *listener*—still not a reader— that he pay attention only to one of the meanings at any given time, listening to it as if to a single story before hearing it again for the second story).[21]

There are other indicators—stylistic, semantic, lexical, and metrical—of Suranna's innovative intention. It is not only a matter of controlling verse to the point where one can use it to write prose. The tone and texture have also changed. Suranna's style is playful, often ironic, reflecting almost with tongue in cheek on preexisting conventions, some of which in any case have lost their force. It is a mistake to read this text too literally. As in the *Kala-purnodayamu*, lovesickness is something of a game (with the inexorable rules of a game).[22] In Telugu the text has a lighthearted, almost parodic quality, especially in those portions of the book that are still heavily indebted to literary conventions. At the same time, a kind of lyrical realism often dominates the narration. Conversations, which comprise a huge part of the narrative, tend to be colloquial and precise. Sucimukhi, in particular, lives up to her name by delivering speeches with the finesse and skill of a diplomat. A certain theatricality is in evidence throughout, not only in the conspicuous case of Pradyumna's performances as Bhadra.[23]

In short, the classic Telugu *kāvya*, as we know it from Peddana onward, has taken a new turn. From this point on, there are basically three possibilities for further evolution. Suranna pioneered the novelistic mode. Bhattu-murti, in his *Vasu-caritramu*—very possibly contemporaneous with Suranna—extended the musicality and bitextuality[24] of Telugu poetry well beyond conventional semantic limits. Later poets explored what is called *citra-kavitva*, a mode of "concrete poetry" that utilizes the graphic potential of the syllables and also eludes a normative semantics.[25] In later centuries, especially in the Telugu-speaking courts of Nayaka-period Tamil Nadu, wholly new genres, indeed an entirely new literary ecology, emerged, rather remote in character from the large-scale, deeply intertextual master-pieces of the sixteenth century.[26]

We cannot follow the course set by Suranna here. The works of his successors, such as the eighteenth-century poet Savaram Cinanarayana-nayaka-kavi's *Kuvalayasva-caritramu*, remain to be studied in depth.[27] There are often, however, surprising resonances that cross great distances, both geographical and temporal. Suranna changed the literary landscape irrevocably; once discovered, the novelistic mode takes on a life of its own. In particular, it becomes difficult to reduce or contain the open-ended, unfinished quality of the novel and the manifold voicing that is so characteristic of its texture. Similarly, there is no retreat from the novel's implicit ontic assertion of the integrity vested in an imagined, heightened inner world—seen to be molding an externality directly known or perceived by the lucid mind. As we have seen, these features are regularly connected to a profoundly self-conscious or reflective stance that generates a certain ironic or playful tone, itself rich in metaphysical implication.

Suranna is not an isolated voice in the cultural continuum of late-medieval South India. We can trace similar developments in Tamil poetry of this period, although the breakthrough to novelistic form was more complete and far reaching in Telugu and more heavily intertextual. There are still many missing links. What can, however, be said with confidence is that Gurajada Appa Rao, at Vizianagaram in northeastern Andhra in the late nineteenth century, took up and explored further the polyphonic, theatrical/novelistic technique in his *Kanyā-śulkamu*.[28] Indeed, Appa Rao is perhaps Suranna's most direct literary descendent, a witness to the continuing vitality of the impulse that we first clearly see in Suranna's poems.[29] The nineteenth-century literary renaissance in Vizianagaram was clearly continuous, on many levels, with the classical apogee of the sixteenth and seventeenth centuries.[30] Still, Gurajada Appa Rao is sometimes said to have articulated, or even invented, a modern consciousness in Andhra. There is much merit to this claim. Perhaps it would, then, be more precise to say that the strong links that bind him to Suranna—who lived some three hundred years before him—attest to the incipient modern character of Suranna's poetic work.

Notes

Preface

1. The following verses have been omitted: 1.59; 2.65–68, 72–74, 78, 80, 101; 4.123; 5.47, 154, 157, 165–66, 170–74, 210, 214.

Introduction

1. New York: Columbia University Press, 2002 and Delhi: Oxford University Press, 2003. The reader is referred to the introduction to that book for further details about Suranna and his time.

2. See our discussion in ibid., 167–71. We are indebted to M. M. Bakhtin, *The Dialogic Imagination*, ed. Michael Holquist (Austin: University of Texas Press, 1981).

3. Reaching its acme in the *Vasu-caritramu* of Bhattu-murti. See the afterword to this volume.

4. See V. Narayana Rao, "Kings, Gods, and Poets: Ideologies of Patronage in Medieval Andhra," and D. Shulman, "Poets and Patrons in Tamil Literature and Literary Legend," in Barbara Stoler Miller (ed.), *The Powers of Art: Patronage in Indian Culture* (Delhi: Oxford University Press, 1992), 142–59 and 89–119; and V. Narayana Rao and D. Shulman, *A Poem at the Right Moment: Remembered Verses from Pre-modern South India* (Berkeley and Los Angeles: University of California Press, 1998).

5. See Velcheru Narayana Rao, David Shulman, and Sanjay Subrahmanyam, *Symbols of Substance: Court and State in Nāyaka-Period Tamil Nadu* (Delhi: Oxford University Press, 1992).

6. See Sanjay Subrahmanyam, *Penumbral Visions: Making Polities in Early Modern South India* (Delhi: Oxford University Press, 2001), 96–98.

7. See Noboru Karashima, *Towards a New Formation: South Indian Society under Vijayanagar Rule* (Delhi: Oxford University Press, 1992), 35–38; Cynthia Talbot, *Precolonial India in Practice: Society, Region and*

111

Identity in Medieval Andhra (New York: Oxford University Press, 2001), 175–207; Phillip B. Wagoner, "Modal Marking of Temple Types in Kakatiya Andhra: Towards a Theory of Decorum for Indian Temple Architecture," in D. Shulman (ed.), *Syllables of Sky: Studies in South Indian Civilization in Honour of Velcheru Narayana Rao* (Delhi: Oxford University Press, 1995), 431–72.

8. Talbot, *Precolonial India*, 192–93.

9. He has close analogues among his contemporaries farther south, in the Tamil country, such as Ativirama Pantiyan and Varatunkarama Pantiyan of Tenkasi, and in sixteenth-century Kerala poets such as Melpattur Narayana Bhatta. Radical literary experimentation, reflecting major shifts in the conceptual basis of south Indian civilization, was widespread throughout the small-scale southern states in the second half of the sixteenth century.

10. As we see already in Krishna-deva-raya's *Amukta-malyada*. Together with Sanjay Subrahmanyam, we are preparing a cultural biography of this king.

11. For the latter, see the afterword to V. Narayana Rao and D. Shulman's, *God on the Hill* (New York: Oxford University Press, 2005); on Lepaksi, see D. Shulman, "Concave and Full: Masking the Mirrored Deity at Lepaksi," in Aditya Malik (ed.), *Günther Sontheimer Memorial Volume*, in press.

12. See Narayana Rao, Shulman, and Subrahmanyam, *Symbols of Substance*, 57–112.

13. The BORI "critical" edition relegates this story, known as *Vajranabha-vadha* (*pradyumnottare*), to an appendix. *Hari-vamsa*, ed. Parashuram Lakshman Vaidya (Poona: Bhandarkar Oriental Research Institute, 1971), App. 29F (pp. 335–64).

14. This idea was not isolated to the literary imagination. In 1398—a century and a half before Suranna—the Bahmani ruler Firuz sent a small band of his soldiers to penetrate the camp of his enemy, Harihara II of Vijayanagara, by assuming the disguise of "strolling performers" (Nilakanta Sastri, *History of South India* [Delhi: Oxford University Press, 1966], 237–38). The infiltrators gave a number of performances, at one of which they killed Harihara's son, the crown prince. Did this incident leave a trace in the collective memory of the Telugu Deccan kingdoms where Suranna lived?

15. In a striking verse in the *Hari-vamsa*, these players, performing a *Ramayana*-drama (*rāmāyaṇaṃ mahākāvyam uddeśaṃ nāṭakī-kṛtam*), are said to have won the approval of the older members of the demon audience, who actually remembered the heroes of the *Ramayana* from personal experience

and could attest to the play's verisimilitude (App. 29F, pp. 248–49: *tat-kāla-jīvino vṛddhā dānavā vismayaṃ gatāḥ / ācacakṣuś ca teṣāṃ vai rūpatulyatvam*).

16. For a detailed discussion of Suranna's narrative departures from the *Hari-vamsa*, see Vemparala Suryanarayana Sastri's introduction to his edition of the text, pp. 17–22; also see, H. S. Kameswar Rao, *A Critical Study of Prabhavati Pradyumna* (Rajahmundry: Vidya Nilaya Printing Works, 1913), 8–16.

CHAPTER I

1. Manmatha, the god of desire, is the son of Vishnu and Lakshmi.

2. Suranna's name has Surana and Suraya (see colophons to the chapters) as variants.

3. On Peki, see the introduction to *Sound of the Kiss*, xix–xx. A *gandharvi* is an immortal, superhuman being, in this case close to a demoness.

4. A *nandaka-stava*, no longer extant.

5. In Surana's village, Krishnarayasamudramu, in the Karnul District; more on this later.

6. A variant form of the same name.

7. This is the plain meaning of verse 39, *pace* Vemparala Suryanarayana Sastri's attempt to identify this Annamma as Surana's sister.

8. Setu = Ramesvaram, where Rama's bridge to Lanka begins.

9. Varuna is the god of the ocean and the western quarter.

10. One of Indra's charming courtesans.

11. See Patanjali, *Mahabhasya* 1.2; Ksetrayya, *Padamulu* (Madras: Vavilla Ramasvamisastrulu and Sons, 1951), 2:73 (*iccina mañcide*). The proverb expresses interdependence, interchangeability, and the vagaries of circumstance.

12. *Brahmacāris*, students attached to the ashram.

13. Vishnu became a dwarf and asked the demon-king Bali for the gift of land—as much as he could cover in three steps. When Bali agreed, the dwarf swelled to the limits of the cosmos.

14. *vipra-vākyaṃ janârdanaḥ*, an aphorism in which Vishnu is quoted as recommending following a Brahmin's advice (at the time of initiating any action). Here Vishnu ironically follows his own advice. Cf. *Kridabhiramamu* of Vinukonda Vallabharaya, 66; Srinatha, *Bhimesvara-puranamu*, 3.41.

15. *upaśruti*—according to Vemparala Suryanarayana Sastri, *upaś-ruti* is a form of divination. One scatters flowers or yellow rice on a

neighbor's house, praises the gods of the house, and then, overhearing whatever is said at that moment inside the house, decides whether he will succeed or not. This is not quite what happens in our text.

16. Literally, Manasa Lake has become like the heart (*mānasa*) of a cruel man, lacking *sārasatva*: good taste, wealth of lotuses.

CHAPTER 2

1. Indra bears a thousand eyes on his body. The sage Gautama cursed the god to carry the marks of a thousand vulvas (because Indra had slept with Gautama's wife, Ahalya), but these marks were converted to eyes to save Indra from indignity.

2. *kavi*—also a water bird. So Indra has spoken truth twice over in the same word.

3. Punning: *viśada-pakṣa-pāti*, a white-winged bird or a person who is partial to what is right.

4. A series of standard similes: Lotus blossoms = feet, crescent moon = toenails, banyan fruits = ankles, tortoise shell = kneecaps, quiver of arrows = calves or shanks, banana plants = thighs, sandbanks = buttocks, whirlpool = navel, lion's waist = waist, golden pots = breasts, lotus stalks = arms, leaf buds = hands, conch = neck, mirrors = cheeks, coral = lips, sesame flower = nose, fish = eyes, bow = eyebrows, piece of the moon = forehead, the letter Sri (written with long sweeping curves in Telugu) = ears, black bees = hair.

5. Bees are said to avoid the *campaka* flower. Poets traditionally compare a woman's nose to this flower.

6. *sthūlârundhatī-nyāya*.

7. *citramahima*—perhaps "skill at painting." Parvati may have painted Prabhavati and then breathed life into the painting.

8. This statement by the goose clarifies an important point. Prabhavati is her mother's daughter but not, in fact, her father's.

CHAPTER 3

1. Apparently Pradyumna had to write the letter in his room in the palace.

2. *ātma-sankalpa-vāsanā-viśeṣa-vaśambunan*. On this highly suggestive phrase, see the discussion in our afterword.

3. Rati is the wife of Manmatha/Ananga, who is Pradyumna in his former life.

4. *Paccigā*—suggesting words that are not considered fit to be shared publicly (sometimes even obscene).

CHAPTER 4

1. *saudha-viṭaṅka-matallika*. Cf. *vīthi-viṭaṅkamu*, "eave."
2. The *pūrva-raṅga*.
3. *gāndhāra-grāma*—a system based on the third note (*ga*). According to Vemparala Suryanarayana Sastri, this music is known only in the world of the gods.
4. A technical list of rhythms follows—the fourteen *madraka-gītas*.
5. Inserted in Sanskrit: *na hi māyāyām asambhāvyam asti*.
6. There is an untranslatable pun: *prabhāvati rohita-kaṇṭakambu*—"O Prabhavati, (your gaze is) a thorn in the eyes of the deer" or, resegmenting, *prabhāva-tirohita-kaṇṭakambu*, "(your gaze) has pulled out the thorns that are enemies by its strength."
7. The goose provides an example: When you call Lakshmi's husband *hari*, it only applies to Vishnu (not to Indra, Yama, or Candra—all acceptable meanings for this word).
8. Airavata, who stands in the eastern direction.
9. *kīlu-gaṇṭu jaḍa*, *solĕmu* (using a circular pad for winding the hair), *vreluḍu kŏppu*, *mūḍu mūlala-bigi-kŏppu* (tied in three places).
10. *maṭṭĕlu*, *pillāṇḍlu*, *vīramaddiyalu*, respectively.
11. *raṅgavallika*.
12. The moon was born out of the ocean of milk, which contains the Vaḍavânala, a fire burning in the shape of a mare's head. The Kālakūṭa poison also emerged when the ocean of milk was churned. The moon is said to approach the sun on new-moon days, and it sits on Siva's head, close to his burning third eye.
13. The *cakora* feeds on both moonlight and fire.
14. Snakes are believed to feed on the wind. The Malaya mountain is filled with snakes, who are attracted to the smell of the sandal trees growing there.

CHAPTER 5

1. Recall that Pradyumna is an incarnation of Manmatha, the god of love, who is married to Rati.
2. Note that these final lines are in the same meter as the letter, as if it were continuing into the narrative.

Afterword

1. See H. S. Kameswar Rao, *A Critical Study of Prabhavati Prady-umna*; but cf. Vemparala Suryanarayana Sastri's introduction to his fine edition with commentary of the *Prabhavati-pradyumnamu*, 34, where he hints at a newly psychologized depiction of love (*mānasika-pravṛttulu*) in this text. Vemparala Suryanarayana Sastri also speaks in terms of *śṛṅgāra-* and *vīra-rasas* (pp. 25–26). Viswanatha Satyanarayana, one of the most penetrating and insightful modern readers of classical Telugu, also recognizes the complexity of Suranna's form of narration, with resulting gain and loss—the gain is that you admire the author's skill as a storyteller, the loss is that you cannot concentrate on any particular *rasa*. "It becomes just a story" (*vaṭṭi katha krinda teli povunu*). Hence, says Satyanarayana, to overcome this fault, Suranna elaborately evokes *śṛṅgāra-rasa* in the last chapter; see introduction to the Emesco edition, xxvii–xxviii.

2. See D. Shulman, "Mirrors and Metaphors in a Tamil Classic," *Hebrew University Studies in Literature* 8 (1980), 224–25.

3. Thus, Krishnadevaraya is supposed to have tied the "anklet of victory" (*gaṇḍa-pĕṇḍĕramu*) to Allasani Peddana's left foot.

4. See 3.59–61.

5. There was a point in the history of Indian poetics where an analogous concept, *bhāvakatva-vyāpāra*, came close to dominating the discourse on aesthetic experience. Bhatta-nayaka, Abhinava-gupta's predecessor, puts forward this concept as a necessary prerequisite for the "enjoyment" (*bhojakatva*) that is the heart of aesthetic pleasure. Perhaps unfortunately, this approach was eventually submerged by Abhinava-agupta's interpretation of *rasa*.

6. *Bhāvanā* is derived from the Sanskrit root *bhū*, to be; more precisely, from the causative root *bhāvaya*, to bring into being.

7. Sucimukhi—the poet's own voice—inspires a remarkable statement (by her interlocutor, Indra) of how poetic language should work: see the opening of chapter 2 (2.3) and our discussion in *Sound of the Kiss*, 167–68.

8. Following closely *Hari-vamsa*, App. 29F, 61–63.

9. We read this Sanskrit line, *na hi māyāyām asambhāvyam asti*, "There's nothing magic cannot do," as an *arthântara-nyāsa*, a generalized conclusion, meant for us as readers.

10. See discussion in Rao, Shulman, and Subrahmanyam, *Symbols of Substance*, 113–24.

11. See section from Peddana's *Manu-caritramu* in V. Narayana Rao and D. Shulman, *Classical Telugu Poetry: An Anthology* (Berkeley and

Los Angeles: University of California Press, 2002), 156–65. *Bhakti* narratives offer some exceptions to this generalization; the god's compassionate presence serves somehow to contain transgression, as when Rukmini elopes with Krishna.

12. Until relatively recently, letters were still sent in this manner in Andhra, with an initial address to the postmaster and a request to deliver the letter to its intended recipient.

13. In this respect—the existence of a split, embedded textual fragment that contains the core of the story—the *Prabhavati-pradyumnamu* is reminiscent of Suranna's other text, the *Kala-purnodayamu*. See Narayana Rao and Shulman, "Invitation to a Second Reading," *Sound of the Kiss*, 203–5.

14. V. Narayana Rao, "Multiple Literary Cultures in Telugu: Court, Temple, and Public," in S. Pollock, *Literary Cultures in History: Reconstructions from South Asia* (Berkeley and Los Angeles: University of California Press, 2003), 391.

15. We have a similar split frame in the prototypical Sanskrit *kāvya*, the *Ramayana*, but without the constant reminder of the addressee's presence: see D. Shulman, *The Wisdom of Poets* (Delhi: Oxford University Press, 2001), 31–34.

16. In the *Hari-vamsa* (App. 29F, 667–94), Prabhavati begs Pradyumna to save himself and gives him the sword with which he will kill her father. However, she also informs him that she has been given a boon by the sage Durvasas to the effect that she will never become a widow. Thus, there is hardly cause for her to be anxious; nor is her choice as pregnant with meaning and feeling as in Suranna's text.

17. This is *Raghava-pandaviyamu* (Madras: Vavilla Ramasvamisastrulu and Sons, 1968), 1.9.

18. Vemparala Suryanarayana Sastri, Introduction, 6.

19. The description applies equally to the armies of Yudhisthira and Dasaratha.

20. For a similar story about Tikkana, see Narayana Rao and Shulman, *Classical Telugu Poetry*, 17–18.

21. *Raghava-pandaviyamu*, *pithika* 18.

22. See Narayana Rao and Shulman, *Sound of the Kiss*, 200–3.

23. Telugu critics rather lamely refer to this quality as *naṭakīyata* while missing the overall tone of comic amusement.

24. We borrow the term from Yigal Bronner's pioneering study of *śleṣa*, "Poetry at its Extreme: The Theory and Practice of Bitextual Poetry in South Asia," Ph.D. dissertation, University of Chicago, 1999.

25. See Narayana Rao, "Multiple Literary Cultures in Telugu," 430–31.

26. See Narayana Rao, Shulman, and Subrahmanyam, *Symbols of Substance*, 171, 292–93, 316–17.

27. We have offered a reading of another novelesque, "psychologizing" *kāvya*, the seventeenth-century *Sarangadhara-caritramu* of Cemakura Venkata-kavi (ibid., 125–43).

28. Velcheru Narayana Rao has prepared a translation of this pivotal work.

29. Twentieth-century modernist Telugu critics, on the other hand, have consistently misunderstood this impulse. As with the *Kala-purnodayamu*, the *Prabhavati-pradyumnamu* suffered the critical depredations of the highly influential C. R. Reddy in his *Kavitva-tattva-vicaramu anu pingali suranarya-krta kala-purnodaya-prabhavati-pradyumnamula vimarsanamu*, first published in 1913 (6th edition; Visakhapatnam: Andhra University Press, 1980). The latter's overly literal readings are suffused with ridicule. He prefers this work to the *Kala-purnodayamu*, but objects to its explicit eroticism and to what he considers unnecessary and illogical artifice (why does Pradyumna need a tunnel to reach Prabhavati when he is such an accomplished magician?). He admires Sucimukhi, the wise negotiator, but is disgusted with the descriptions of Prabhavati's physical beauty, longings for Pradyumna, and, even worse, with her preferring her husband to her father. We would be glad to be able to say that C. R. Reddy's views are now passé, but this is unfortunately not the case.

30. We are preparing a complete study of the Vizianagaram courtly production.

Index

Note: We have not marked names and titles with diacritics in the body of the text or the notes. All such forms appear in the index with standard diacritic marking.